# DEATH
## FROM
# ABOVE

**a supernatural thriller**

**Mark Polino**

Mark Polino/Resistor Media
mpolino@mpolino.com
www.mpolino.com

Publisher's Note: This is a work of fiction. Names, characters, places, and incidents are a product of the author's imagination. Locales and public names are sometimes used for atmospheric purposes. Any resemblance to actual people, living or dead, or to businesses, companies, events, institutions, or locales is completely coincidental.

Book Layout & Design ©2013 - BookDesignTemplates.com
Cover by Anne Claire Williams
Rear cover art © kudinovart used with permission via fotolia.com

Ordering Information:
Quantity sales. Special discounts are available on quantity purchases by corporations, associations, and others. For details, contact the "Special Sales Department" at the address above.

Death From Above / Mark Polino. -- 1st edition

ISBN-13: 978-0692235324 (Resistor Media)

ISBN-10: 0692235329

To Angelina,

*Of my children, you are the reader, so this book
is for you.*

*If this turns into a movie, the dedication goes to
Alex.*

*When they make a video game from it, I'll
dedicate it to Micah.*

# Prologue

FROM THE TOP OF THE TEMPLE dedicated to Q'uq'umatz, the high priest Ajk'ín Kan Ek' looked out over the great Mayan city of Ox Te' Tuun. Below him, the people had been whipped into a hypnotic frenzy. They were chanting in unison, calling for blood. The ceremony was almost finished, but Ajk'ín Kan Ek' knew that it wouldn't be enough. The oracles had foreseen the death of the empire. The great city-state of Ox Te' Tuun was past its prime. The glory years a distant memory. The prophets said that the city's slow decay could not be stopped. Ajk'ín Kan Ek' would finish the ceremony and then move to protect the treasures of Q'uq'umatz for future generations.

Slowly Ajk'ín Kan Ek' raised his hands. The crowd went silent. On the thirteen stone altars knelt thirteen prisoners, captured from the neighboring kingdom of Tikal. Behind the first group were lines of prisoners twelve deep, one line for each altar, yielding a total of 169. Numbers were important in the religion of the Maya, and Ajk'ín Kan Ek' had calculated that this level of sacrifice was the only chance to save the kingdom from the disrepair it was slipping into. Even if it failed, he hoped that the massive bloodletting would ease his troubled mind, at least for a little while.

From above the prisoners, Ajk'ín Kan Ek' looked down at the sacred text. This above all else must be preserved. Rising slightly on his toes, Ajk'ín Kan Ek' dropped his hands. Simultaneously, priests plunged thirteen stone knives into the prisoners. The crowd roared in jubilation at the deaths, drunk on power and blind to the decay of their society. This gruesome display was repeated again and again. By the end, the altars and floors were slippery with blood making the last few executions sloppy. Prisoners died slowly, sometimes flopping off the altars, only to be hunted down and butchered by the priests. When it was finally over, Ajk'ín Kan Ek' dismissed the crowd to wander home tired and punch drunk from the long ceremony.

Deep in the bowels of the great flat top pyramid, Ajk'ín Kan Ek' prepared the hiding place for the book of the feathered serpent god Q'uq'umatz. The book of Q'uq'umatz had been protected by priests for more than a thousand years. He might be the last of those priests, but he would do his duty.

A special chamber had been built, and now Ajk'ín Kan Ek' placed the book on the chamber's altar. Servants sealed him in from outside. Ajk'ín Kan Ek' then blocked the chamber entrance from within. Slowly, he chanted from memory the ancient curse of protection found in the middle of the book, "Death from above to those who disturb the book of Q'uq'umatz." Shaking with fear and anticipation, he sealed the curse with blood when he plunged the stone knife deep into his chest.

# 1.

THE TROPICAL HEAT WAS OPPRESSIVE, but the humidity was indescribable. The air conditioning in the Raintree family's rented Chevy simply couldn't keep up with the Mexican summer.

"How much longer until we get there?"

The day had just started and Ferdinand was already whining.

"It won't be long now," replied his mother Allegra.

"That's what you said an hour ago," replied Ferdinand's twin, Sebastian. "I wish we had stayed at the hotel. I don't want to see some stupid ruin. If it was any good it wouldn't be 'ruined'.

Allegra rolled her eyes while the twins pouted. "What about the howler monkeys outside the room this morning? They were pretty cool weren't they?"

Both boys shrugged. The monkeys had been pretty cool, but they weren't going to give their mom the satisfaction of admitting it.

The Raintrees, Richard, Allegra and their 12 year old twin boys, Ferdinand and Sebastian, had come to Mexico for history, not for the hotels and beaches. They were eco-tourists looking to explore the wild ruins of the Mayan city of Calakmul.

Richard was an adjunct professor of literature at the University of New Mexico. Tall, thin, and a little frumpy, he had settled nicely into the college professor role. Allegra ran a global warming website and newsletter with a small but zealous following. Allegra was shorter and rounder than her husband and well...somewhat top heavy. So far, the twins were rounder, more like their mother, but she had hopes that their new vegan diet would fix that.

After flying to Cancun from their home in Albuquerque, they had driven three hundred miles to the Hotel Puerta Calakmul, on the edge of the Calakmul Biosphere Preserve. Their hotel was a series of bungalows nestled among the rain forest. It was not rustic, in the sense that it had electricity and amenities, but it was very disconnected. With only a common TV and internet room for the whole facility, the boys had quickly grown bored.

This morning they had left early for the tedious drive to the ancient city. In the 1990's, the Mexican government had finally built a road to the site making the trip marginally easier. The narrow, winding, thirty-seven mile road was hard on the car and even harder on the driver. As they approached the site, Allegra felt the need to give the twins one last warning.

"Boys," she began. "Calakmul was a very important city. In ancient times it was known as Ox Te' Tuun and housed more than fifty thousand people. This isn't a touristy ruin like Chichen Itza and it's not a fake pyramid like Disney World. There's no gift shop, no visitor's center and no railings. The archeologists are slowly peeling back the jungle, but even now, many structures have not been fully explored. It is very important that you be careful and not take anything you find at the site. Also, it's going to be very hot. You have water in your backpacks, please drink a lot today. Remember, take nothing but pictures, and leave nothing but footprints." Her voice rose an octave in excitement as she quoted one of her favorite phrases.

The boys rolled their eyes and snickered in the back seat. Allegra had the annoying habit of talking in clichés, as if she had few original thoughts of her own. The twins looked at each other and silently decided to do whatever they wanted. After all, it's not like their parents were going to drag them back to the hotel any time soon.

Richard Raintree grumbled as he paid for the third time. He had already paid the local ejido for access to road, and he had paid again to enter the biosphere preserve. Now he had to pay one more time to enter the ruins. Richard pulled the rental into the makeshift dirt parking lot. The lot was on a small rise above the valley. The city sat below them on a plateau surrounded by marsh. Richard drew a deep breath and let out a low whistle as he glimpsed the top half of a grayish white pyramid rising more than a hundred and eighty feet in the air. Calakmul was littered with more than a thousand structures in just the city core, but the magnificent white pyramid, known antiseptically as Structure II, stood out from among the rest.

A small mini-bus was there to take tourists and researchers from the parking lot down to the site.

There was only one other tourist on their bus and only a handful wandering around the city.

The hotel had arranged for a local guide, a boy not much older than the twins, to lead the Raintree family through the ruin. The path through the jungle from the bus stop was uneven and steep, though not particularly treacherous. As they walked down, the jungle suddenly parted and the monstrous, gray-white pyramid of Structure II lay in front of them. It took their breath away. The pyramids were huge. The city was huge. It was hard to understand how a city this large had been found in the early 1930's and then forgotten about for almost fifty years.

Structure II had steps running up its height, with periodic breaks for wide platforms. "The government just started allowing people to explore inside the estructura dos," the guide explained. "But it can be dangerous. Please do not hurt yourself," he continued in broken English. "The interior is open until dark. There are some lanterns inside, but you really need flashlights."

If the guide thought he would have a short day because they didn't have flashlights, he had underestimated Allegra. The boy scouts weren't good enough for her children, too old fashioned. She'd enrolled the twins in an eco-scout program; a progressive alternative to the Boy Scouts focused on saving the planet. They still managed to get the 'be prepared' part right. Each of the Raintrees pulled a flashlight with fresh batteries from their backpack.

The family hiked through the city and climbed the steep stone steps of Structure II. By the time they reached the first level, Richard was puffing hard. The twins fared better, but about half way up, even they had to bend over and use their hands to keep from falling. Breathless, they reached the top and looked out over the valley. Ferdinand looked down and nudged Sebastian. He pointed to a set of weathered stone tables a level below them.

"Do you think that's where they sacrificed the virgins?" he asked.

"We'll go down later and find out," was the answer.

At the top of the pyramid sat a nine room palace with space for food preparation, sleeping quarters, and ceremonial purposes. Even in the dim light everyone marveled at the brightly colored paintings on the temple walls. Richard and Allegra moved slowly through the structure looking carefully at each glyph.

"This was believed to be the palace of the ruler of Calakmul," their guide said. "The roped off cutout in the floor held a specially prepared tomb that has

been moved to the Museo Nacional de An-
tropología. It is believed to hold the remains of Calakmul's greatest ruler, Jaguar Claw."

At this the twins looked at each other. They silently agreed that Jaguar Claw was a pretty cool
name for a king.

"Calakmul warred for years with a rival city to the
south, Tikal. In the next room..."

The boys quickly lost interest. "Mom," asked Sebastian, "can we explore inside?"

Allegra answered absentmindedly, absorbed in a
particularly interesting glyph. "Sure dear, be careful.
Oh, and take your backpacks and drink your water."

The twins climbed down a level to the stone tables they had seen from the top. Imagining virgins
being sacrificed here was cool for about a minute.
"I'm bored," they said in unison turning toward each
other. That made them laugh. The boys climbed
lower and moved into the interior. A rope cordoned
off a tunnel that was marked with a sign in English
and Spanish indicating that this section of the pyramid was off limits. Without hesitating, the boys
ducked under the rope.

The restricted section of the pyramid was obviously being prepared for further exploration. The
paintings on the walls weren't as bright. A thin layer
of dust covered everything. Half built sections of

scaffolding lined the walls, along with buckets full of brushes and sponges. The boys stopped at a particularly interesting section of the wall. It depicted a winged serpent god devouring a village in vivid detail.

"That's what I'm talking about," said Ferdinand, excitedly pointing toward the glyph.

"Eh, it just looks like they ripped off the Aztecs."

Both of the boys were jaded. They'd been on a number of these trips, including one to Chichen Itza two years ago. What they really wanted to do was dump the jungle and go to the beach for jet skis and parasailing.

The twins turned on their flashlights and moved deeper into the gloom. The tunnel turned a corner and they moved into the heart of Structure II. Deep in the pyramid, lanterns were few and far between. The only illumination came from their flashlights. The dark murkiness of the interior settled on the boys. Neither twin wanted to admit to being scared so they kept moving.

Sebastian's flashlight illuminated a dim wall painting. One section showed a virgin sacrifice. Another depicted lines of what looked like prisoners being executed. In each case, the sky god from earlier was eating their remains.

"Now that is pretty cool." It was Sebastian this time.

"You just think the virgins are cool," Ferdinand responded.

"No, I think girls with their clothes off are cool."

Puberty had hit Sebastian hard earlier in the year. Ferdinand hadn't quite caught up yet. He dragged Sebastian farther down the tunnel. Their flashlight beams stopped at a rock slide. It looked like an earthquake had taken down part of the ceiling and wall.

"Crap," said Sebastian. "All this for a pile of rocks."

Ferdinand stepped up and pulled a softball sized rock out of the pile. He started tossing it in his hand. "Well, what do you want to do now? I'm bored again."

Sebastian picked out a rock too. "Well, I don't want to go back and see mom and dad." He threw his rock back down the tunnel. It bounced and echoed off the far wall.

Ferdinand threw his rock next. After that it became a game. Who could throw the farthest? Could they hit the far wall without bouncing? How many times could they skip a rock before hitting the end of the tunnel? It went on like that for twenty minutes.

Ferdinand pulled a rock from the pile and it started a small rock slide. The boys jumped back. "Now look what you did," Sebastian mocked.

Ferdinand shined his flashlight at the mess he had made. As he tried to figure out if he could put some of the rocks back, he saw a void that had not been there before. He moved his flashlight around and found that they had actually opened up a small hole into a chamber behind the rock slide. The pile of rocks wasn't nearly as thick as it appeared and there was an empty space behind the rocks.

"Holy shit," said Ferdinand when he saw the hole. He started pulling at rocks to widen the opening.

Sebastian was more reticent. "Um Ferd, do you really think that's a good idea? You could pull the wall down on top of us."

"I think there's something else back here. Come on, help me move these rocks. It could be a treasure room!"

"It could also be full of booby traps. You have seen Indiana Jones haven't you?"

Ferdinand didn't stop, so Sebastian reluctantly started moving rocks too. After a few minutes they had a hole that they could just squeeze through. The wall around it looked pretty unsteady though.

"I'm going in," announced Ferdinand.

"I'm not," reiterated Sebastian.

"What's the matter, you don't want to find the treasure?"

"No, I want to live long enough to touch a pair of boobies."

What is it with him and boobies all of sudden thought Ferdinand. "Fine, you can wait outside while I go in. That way you can call for help if I get stuck or hit by a giant rolling boulder."

Sebastian liked that idea because it didn't make him seem like a chicken. If Ferdinand got hurt he could be a hero.

Ferdinand slipped off his backpack and crawled in the hole. It was tight, but he managed not to get stuck. Inside, he stood up and shined his flashlight around. As he panned the light around the room, the beam caught a skeleton leaning against the far wall. Ferdinand jumped back and yelled, dropping the flashlight and tripping in the process. The light landed on the floor and spun. It came to rest shining on a stone altar set in the middle of the room.

"Are you okay?" hollered Sebastian.

"Yeah. I just dropped my flashlight."

Slowly, shakily, Ferdinand got to his feet. He picked up the flashlight and saw that there was something on top of the altar. Willing himself to ignore the skeleton for now, he moved to the altar. On top of it he found a book.

The book was about eight inches high and decorated with colored images that were still bright after all of these years. It looked like an ancient comic book. Ferdinand started to lift up the book, then he remembered the Indiana Jones movies he'd watched.

He nudged the book with his flashlight. It moved. He pushed it to the end of the altar. So far, so good, he thought. No poison darts or shooting spears. Just to be safe, he pushed the book completely off the altar and on to the stone floor. He waited hardly breathing. Nothing happened. With a sense of relief, Ferdinand gingerly picked up the book.

He expected it to be dry and brittle like other old documents his parents had dragged him to see, but it wasn't. The book was smooth and soft, almost like it was brand new.

As he lifted the book, Ferdinand's hair stood on end. He felt very nervous. Gently, he laid the book back down on to the altar and moved to examine the rest of the room.

The skeleton was slumped against a wall. A stone knife was wedged between the ribs. The sense of foreboding passed when he put the book down and now his courage was back. Well, I know how he died, thought Ferdinand. I wonder if he got here first and found the booby trap. Any clothing had rotted away, so Ferdinand couldn't guess how long the skeleton had been there. It was creepy seeing a skeleton, but now that he wasn't scared, he was ready to move on.

Sebastian called to him and a light shined into the entrance hole. "Hey, are you ok? Is there treasure in there?"

"No treasure yet, but I'm still looking. Give me a minute."

The walls held more paintings of the winged, snake-like sky god. There were more paintings of virgins. Great. If I tell Sebastian I'll never get him out of here, he thought. He searched the whole chamber and was disappointed to find that there really wasn't any treasure. Ferdinand searched again looking for a secret passageway that might lead to a treasure room. Not finding anything, he ended up back at the center of the room staring at the altar.

He pushed and pulled on the sides of the altar. He placed the book on the floor and pushed on the top. Ferdinand pressed every brick individually, but nothing happened.

"How much longer are you going to be?" Sebastian whined.

"I'm coming."

Ferdinand picked up the book to put it back on the altar, and then he changed his mind. If there wasn't any treasure in here he might as well get something for his little adventure. He wasn't sure why he didn't tell Sebastian about the book, he just didn't. He simply tucked it in the back of his pants, covered it with his shirt, and crawled out of the hole.

"Are you okay?" asked Sebastian as Ferdinand climbed out of the hole.

"Yeah, there was just some old dead guy in there." Ferdinand tried to sound nonchalant, but he was shaking. The sense of nervousness was back. "Let's get out of here."

Sebastian led the way through the darkness. Behind him, Ferdinand slipped the book into his backpack. Outside in the sunlight, Ferdinand's nervousness vanished, and he described the room, the skeleton, the knife, and the altar. He intentionally made no mention of the book.

That night, Ferdinand carried his backpack into the hotel bathroom and locked the door. He pulled out the book that he had found. It was an odd book, not bound but folded, like a really long pamphlet. There were no words, just pictures. His first thought was that this was an ancient comic book, but they didn't really have comic books back then did they? So this must have just been a regular book. Sitting on the toilet he flipped through it.

The pictures were bright and sharp. They were similar to the wall paintings in the pyramid. He wondered if the book really was old or if it was some kind of tourist replica. Ferdinand dismissed the thought. There was no way a tourist book would end up in a cave like that with a dead guy.

As he looked through the book, he found that he could interpret the scenes. They made sense to him. He could read it. He was a genius. Maybe he would be a world famous archeologist when he grew up. He could be the next Indiana Jones. He could date Lara Croft. Where did that thought come from? Back to the book.

Ferdinand opened the book and started reading in earnest. This was the sacred text of Q'uq'umatz, the feathered snake god of the Maya, lord of wind, rain, and sky, the co-creator of humanity and, Ferdinand gulped nervously, he had just stolen his book. He quit reading. Ferdinand was suddenly very, very scared. Scared enough that he might pee his pants. Fortunately, he was sitting in the right room for that.

* * *

Two days later, the Raintree family was sunburned from their time at Calakmul and their days spent trekking through the surrounding jungle. Ferdinand didn't have much time to himself so he did his best to forget about the book. Sunday came and it was time for the family to fly home. The worn out group shuffled aboard Fiesta Air flight 169 for the flight home to Albuquerque.

The Fiesta Air Boeing 737 had seen better days. Even the sombrero on the tail looked tired and worn. The plane had been retired from Southwest Airline's fleet after a long, hard life before joining Fiesta Air. Fiesta was trying to build a discount airline by flying into Mexican tourist spots from targeted cities in the southwest United States. News reports of Mexican drug violence had almost grounded them. The airline was headed for bankruptcy when they discovered the eco-tourism market.

Fiesta retooled to pair trips to Cancun with rainforest excursions and overnight camping in Mayan ruins. They sold the trips at inflated prices and marketed complete packages in cities with a large number of environmentally concerned citizens. Fiesta also partnered with a number of high profile environmental groups to improve their standing. To ensure that they made money, Fiesta cut back on maintenance and crammed even more seats into a 737 than Southwest did. They then charged for every little item, even on all inclusive packages.

The Raintrees sat just ahead of the wing with Ferdinand at the window, Sebastian in the middle and Allegra on the aisle. Richard sat across the aisle with his knees crushed against the seat in front of him.

Despite his discomfort, Richard was asleep before the plane ever taxied. The 737 took off to the southeast and then turned north for the three and a half hour flight to Albuquerque. Ferdinand looked to his right. Sebastian was playing games on his iPod touch, Allegra was engrossed in her iPad, and Richard was snoring. Quietly, Ferdinand slipped out the book and turned toward the window to hide it.

He examined it again. His hands were shaking. The sacred text of Q'uq'umatz was a mixture of pictures and symbols. As before, Ferdinand realized that he could understand the symbols. The book seemed to only be about a hundred pages long, but it wasn't bound. The paper was thick and yellow and had obviously stood up to thousands of years of being folded. Despite its age, it felt fragile and yet sturdy at the same time. Even with its relatively short length, Ferdinand was engrossed. He started again at the beginning. Half an hour later, he realized that the symbols and pictures provided a deeper meaning than would have been found in printed text. The book may have only been a hundred pages long, but it contained the equivalent of thousands of pages about the Maya and their sky god. When the captain announced two hours later that they had crossed into the United States, Ferdinand didn't hear a thing he said.

As they approached the three hour point, Fiesta Air flight 169 was high over west Texas and about to begin it's descent toward Albuquerque. Ferdinand was only halfway through the text of Q'uq'umatz. The section he was reading contained a curse. He interpreted the symbols as "To those who would disturb the book of Q'uq'umatz shall come death from above." Ferdinand shuttered along with the plane.

Turning his head to the left, Ferdinand looked out the window at the wing. He watched in horror as rivets popped off from the wing and were sucked back into the slipstream. Ferdinand was paralyzed. It was like watching a car crash or a train wreck. He couldn't look away. He couldn't even nudge Sebastian. Ferdinand watched in horror as the left wing separated from the plane with a terrifying screech of wrenching metal. The stress on the wing and weight of the engine was too much. The wing ripped loose from the plane and fell behind into the slipstream. Immediately the Boeing 737 rolled to the right, pulled by the weight of the right wing and the remaining engine. Fiesta Air flight 169 tumbled thirty-two thousand feet toward the west Texas prairie.

The Boeing 737 took nearly three terrifying minutes to cartwheel into the ground. The violence of the spin caused the overhead bins to open. The flying luggage mercifully knocked many of the passengers unconscious. Those who weren't so lucky screamed, prayed, and grabbed at their loved ones in terror. Oxygen masks dropped from the ceiling and passengers flailed trying to put them on as the plane rolled. A flight attendant careened off of the bulkhead violently, collapsing into a heap in on the floor.

When the spin started, there was a man in the lavatory. He was bounced around like clothes in a dryer...a violent, bloody dryer. Passengers threw up, adding their vomit to the rotating mess. Others watched as a woman who was not buckled in flipped onto the ceiling and was then unceremoniously dumped onto a row of seats, breaking her back. The pilots wrestled with the controls, but they never really had a chance to save the aircraft. Planes without wings do not fly.

As the plane spun, Ferdinand was left with one last thought, "It's all my fault."

Two minutes and fifty-three seconds after the left wing sheared off, the Boeing 737, with a hundred and sixty souls on board, slammed unceremoniously into the triangle formed by the cities of Midland, San Angelo, and Stockton, Texas.

# 2.

JENNIFER LYNCH'S MORNING RUN through the North Atlanta suburb of Sandy Springs, Georgia was a three mile loop that took her past the Cox buildings on Peachtree-Dunwoody road and left on Hammond. As she turned down Perimeter Center, she passed the offices of the Atlanta Journal and Constitution and finally jogged toward home via Central Parkway. The trim, twenty-eight year old blonde struggled to keep to her running schedule because her job kept her on the road way too much. A mechanical engineering graduate from Georgia Tech, Jennifer Lynch worked as an investigator for the National Transportation and Safety Board, specializing in aircraft investigations.

Commonly abbreviated NTSB, one of the board's primary mandates was the investigation of airplane crashes in the United States. Jennifer had the duty as a "go team" member this week. Despite her mechanical engineering degree, her specialty was Air Traffic Control. Her father was an air traffic controller with the Federal Aviation Administration, and she had all but grown up in a control tower.

The NTSB investigates roughly two thousand aircraft incidents a year and yet it had been more than ten years since the last major airliner crash in the United States. Military planes crashed. Private planes went down. Even regional jets affiliated with the big airlines crashed. It was rare, but it happened. Big jets occasionally went down in other parts of the world too. In the United States, however, large jets just didn't crash with any regularity, so it was the smaller crashes, near misses and other incidents that kept them busy.

Jennifer made the last major turn on her run and headed home with the sound of Tat's Road to Paradise pounding through her headphones. On her hip, her pager buzzed. Though pagers had long since gone out of style, the NTSB still used them to notify go teams. The NTSB is a small government agency with less than six hundred employees. Its budget is almost a rounding error. No one was willing to spend money on a more modern system when the one they had not only worked, but was cheap. Jennifer jogged in place as she checked her pager. There had been a crash and she'd been activated.

Jennifer sprinted home. Despite being on twenty four hour alert, Go Team members don't keep a bagged packed because they never know where a crash could occur. Packing for a military crash in the desert is significantly different from dressing for a forest service incident in Alaska. They do, however, keep a technical bag with flashlights, voice recorders, cameras, specialty equipment, and lots of tape always at the ready.

In her apartment, Jennifer put her voice mail on speaker as she started pulling off her clothes. She heard Go Team lead Ed Rollins. "Jen, we're activated. A Fiesta Air 737 crashed near Midland, Texas. This one looks bad. No early reports of survivors. Get on the first flight to Midland-Odessa. We'll have someone meet you."

"Shit," breathed Jennifer. Small crashes were bad, this was going to be terrible. She might go days without a shower, so she grabbed a fast one. As she packed, she checked the weather. Midland was showing typical west Texas summer climate, hot with little chance of rain. That's something, she thought. Rain had a nasty tendency to wash away evidence. Plus it made life miserable for the investigators. Jennifer pulled on cargo shorts and a tank top. A large blue button down went over that plus hiking boots to complete the look. She looked more like a hiker in a national park than an NTSB agent, but it was hard to look good while traipsing around looking for bodies and airplane parts. Bags in hand she ran outside to meet a car to take her to the airport.

At Atlanta's Hartsfield-Jackson airport, the next flight to Midland-Odessa was via AmerAir through Dallas-Fort Worth. As an NTSB agent, Lynch had priority on any flight she wanted. That priority only applied to getting on the flight, it didn't extend to her seat. She settled uncomfortably into a middle seat near the back of a Boeing 737. Her seat mate on the aisle couldn't fit between the armrests. Nothing like rubbing up against a fat man for the next three hours, she thought.

The 737 Jennifer flew on wasn't much newer than the one than the one that had gone down. She wasn't a nervous flyer, but today she didn't appreciate the irony. She was flying to investigate the crash of a plane very similar to the one she was on. Jen looked around trying to take it all in. The plane on the ground would look very different.

As they took off, Jen tried to steel herself for what she was about to experience. No initial reports of survivors was a bad sign, but those reports could be wrong. A compact crash site could be good or bad. There was less searching for parts, but you could end up with everything pancaked together. That made identification and investigation a lot harder. Jen closed her eyes and tried to catch sleep that wouldn't come.

\* \* \*

On the ground in Texas, Jennifer surveyed the primary crash site. It was surprisingly compact. The plane had literally fallen out of the sky and created a small crater in an empty field. Drainage ditches ran parallel to a two lane road bordering one side of the field. Egress is going to be a problem here, Jen thought. They would need heavy equipment and she hoped the road would support it. Big crashes meant big go teams and most of the team was already there. Jennifer moved to find Ed Rollins.

Ed was in his early fifties. He'd been investigating crashes for twenty-five years. Lynch was the youngest member of the go team and this would be her first major airliner crash. Ed wasn't quite old enough to be her father, but looked out for her like one.

"This one is bad Jen," Ed started without bothering with a greeting. "Effectively zero chance of finding any survivors. We're still working to secure the scene. I need you on the east side with Murphy tagging and photographing items."

Jennifer hoisted her bag with her camera and other supplies and headed east looking for Ted Murphy. She found him inserting a small red wire flag next to a mangled body.

It doesn't really matter what a team member's specialty is, in the hours after a crash everyone is focused on a finding a short list of things. Survivors are first on that list, remains are second, and every little piece of the aircraft is third. In the coming weeks they would effectively put this plane back together in a hangar somewhere like a gruesome jigsaw puzzle. Each piece would be important in finding out why Fiesta Air flight 169 crashed.

Every airport has a stash of NTSB crash supplies tucked away in a shed somewhere. Midland-Odessa airport was the closest so they got the call. The supplies had beaten Jen to the scene and she grabbed a pile of flags on her way to find Murph. Red flags indicated bodies. Green marked injured passengers ready to be moved. Yellow flags were for the injured who couldn't be moved and blue flags were used for important discoveries, like the aircraft's black boxes.

Ted Murphy looked up from placing a red flag next to a body. The face of an elderly woman looked blankly back at Jen. The woman's torso was intact, but there was nothing but a bloody mess from the waist down. Ted stood up as Jennifer approached.

Murphy was a retired Boeing engineer. He'd made as much money as a consultant in the ten years since his early retirement as he had during his thirty years at Boeing. More companies were getting into the private jet business and private jet makers were pushing into the commercial aircraft space. Murphy was riding this wave of high demand for experienced aviation engineers.

Ever since engineering school at Embry-Riddle he'd been teased about his last name. With engineers' almost universal love of Murphy's Law, a guy named Murphy wasn't going to get off easy. After he left Boeing, he'd done some consulting for NTSB and signed on as a structural expert, willing to assist in the event of a crash. He'd spent his life with people telling him things may go wrong, he thought he might as well investigate why.

Murphy was in his sixties, dark haired, with a paunch. Every time he worked a crash he swore it was his last. He was getting too old to go traipsing around in fields, but every time the pager went off, he answered the call.

"Hi Jen," Ted started. "This crash is really ugly. This lady got lucky. We're at least going to be able to identify her remains. That's probably not true for half of the passengers. This was a tourist flight from Cancun so there were a lot of sunburned people and a lot of kids on board."

"What do we know?" Jen asked.

"The plane went in wing first and rolled, almost bounced, splitting off both the tail and the nose. We're still looking for the other wing and we haven't found the black boxes. I started over by that ditch," he pointed indicating a drainage ditch dug in to the clay soil, "and moved north. If you'll move south we should get some additional help soon. The ground is bone dry and there's no sign of rain for the rest of week, so that should help. The outer rim of the site is pretty safe. The area near the fuselage will probably require full hazmat suits. It's crushed so badly I think we're going to have to cut our way in."

Jen groaned at the thought of using a hazardous materials suit in the west Texas heat. Still, an airplane is full of hazardous material and she had no desire to breathe high concentrations of jet fuel, hydraulic fluid, and possible blood borne pathogens. Jen said thanks and grabbed her gear. She setup a search pattern in her head using the ditch as a reference point. The Holy Grail right now was the two "black boxes" from flight 169. These were the Flight Data Recorder (FDR) and the Cockpit Voice Recorder (CVR). They weren't actually black, but bright orange to aid detection. Each was roughly the size of a car battery. The CVR is basically a rugged tape recorder that records the pilot and copilot's communication. The FDR is similar, but it records flight status inputs like changes in altitude or deploying the flaps. These instruments would provide information about was going on in the cockpit and with the aircraft's systems in the period leading up to the crash. They were critical to determining what went wrong.

* * *

Lynch trudged through the dry clay and low grass. She knelt down and used a red flag to mark a hand that had somehow been thrown from the aircraft. She had been told that you saw all kinds of strange things in airliner crashes. Things like the passengers strapped to their seats without a mark on their bodies, but still dead as can be. There were stories of decapitations from flying carry-on luggage, seats coming loose and bouncing around aircraft with passengers still strapped to them and the occasional, miraculous passenger who walked away from a catastrophic crash without a scratch. There won't be any of those today, she thought.

Jennifer worked her grid. After the hand, she found parts of the plane's tail that had flown off on impact. Then she moved to a larger piece of debris that stuck out away from the main wreckage. It turned out to be a section of three seats upside down in the grass. The passengers were still strapped in. Jen took her time marking and photographing the seats. No one would be unbuckling from this row. She made the mistake of flipping the seat over. The corpse on one end was a man. Well, she thought it was man. The corpse's head was missing. A woman was strapped into the seat on the other side. Her face had caved in like a melon.

It was the seat in the middle that was the worst. The center seat held a little girl of about six or seven. She was wearing a Disney Princess t-shirt and clutching a Winnie the Pooh stuffed animal. The force of the impact had thrown her against the seat belt hard enough to cut her in two. When Jennifer flipped back the seat the little girl's lower torso slid out of the seat belt and onto the ground. Jennifer gagged involuntarily and spun to the side where she threw up until she had nothing left. She gave a final, retching heave and wiped her mouth on the back of her hand. Great, she thought. Now I have to tag and mark my puke.

Jennifer worked her way closer to the wrecked tail when a glimpse of orange caught her eye. She moved through grass and there it was, the flight data recorder. Jen called it in. The experts would want to get this to the lab in Washington D.C. as fast as possible. As she bent down to mark the FDR with a blue flag she saw something in the grass next to it. It looked like a book.

Jen bent down to look at it. The odd looking book was perfectly preserved. There wasn't a burn mark or a dirt smudge on it. Funny, she thought. There was no title, no author, in fact, no words on it at all. She marked it with a blue flag, photographed its position, and picked it up. She wasn't going anywhere until the team came to pick up the FDR. She might as well examine this unusual item while she waited.

The odd book was like nothing she had ever seen. It unfolded like a big pamphlet. There were no words, no title, just pictures. It looked old, very, very old. What was it doing on that plane? Minutes later, a team came running up to take possession of the FDR. Jen noted where she had found the book, bagged it, and threw it into her duffel. She would add it to the list of items found later.

* * *

The NTSB team held a recap each night to cover what had been found. Jennifer had continued processing the scene until Ed had finally called them in. They could bring in lights to work in the dark, but since there were no survivors, he didn't see a need to burn out the team.

Back in the hotel, Jen showered and started making calls to the FAA. After a late dinner, the group gathered in a conference room at the Hampton Inn that they had commandeered. Ed Rollins started them off.

"Look everyone, I know it's been a long day and you're all tired so we'll try to be quick. We've made good progress today in finding the pieces of Fiesta Air 169. Both the cockpit voice recorder and the flight data recorder are on their way to Washington, so let's recap what we know and get some sleep. Easy stuff first. Weather?"

"Weather was not a factor. Clear skies from Cancun to Albuquerque. No reports of turbulence from any other aircraft along the route. This simply wasn't weather," said Brandon Herman. Brandon was a certified consulting meteorologist who worked for the National Oceanic and Atmospheric Administration (NOAA). NOAA loaned him to the NTSB as needed for crash related weather help.

"Next up, survival factors," Ed continued.

A Dr. Renteria responded. "Based on the way that this plane went in there was zero chance of survival. I'll let structural tackle the details, but we found the missing wing several miles away. It's my professional opinion that this flight couldn't be saved. "

"Thank you doctor. Flight Control?"

Jennifer was up. "Fiesta Air 169 was on a properly filed flight plan. This was a regularly scheduled route. The pilots correctly notified Houston control on entering U.S. airspace. The plane was following its flight plan and responding to controllers. At 6 pm local time, Midland controllers registered a mayday from flight 169 indicating that they had lost control of the airplane. Subsequent attempts to contact the aircraft were unsuccessful.

The closest other aircraft was sixty miles ahead of Fiesta 169. Another plane was seventy-five miles behind. Midland tower showed the aircraft in level flight at cruising altitude, thirty-two thousand feet, before the Mayday. The aircraft was due to start it's descent at any moment. At that height, they couldn't have run into a small plane. Midland had one private jet on final approach and no other traffic in the area. Also, we haven't found any evidence of another aircraft in the wreckage. The boxes will give us more, but this wasn't an air traffic control problem."

The briefing continued with Flight Operations. They were still going through the crew records, but so far, nothing pointed toward crew. Crew rest had been within the required parameters. The pilots were experienced and had no history of drinking. Nothing stood out.

Systems was going to need some time to sort out hydraulics, pneumatics, and flight controls. The FDR would help. Their big need was time.

"Power plant?"

"The left engine suffered a catastrophic shutdown when the left portion of the wing separated from the aircraft. It's very, very early, but we believe that the engine shutdown was a result of the separation of the wing, not the other way around." Josh Benson was a former Pratt and Whitney engineer who could literally take apart a jet engine, put it back together, and then calmly fly on the plane it was attached to. If he had decided that it wasn't the engine, then it wasn't the engine.

Ed stood up. "All right, let's address the elephant in the room, Structure." He pointed to Murphy.

Murphy stood up. "The left wing, engine and all, separated from the fuselage. We found it five miles from the crash site. Catastrophic separation could send the plane into an uncontrolled spin caused by the weight of the remaining wing. Right now we think that's what happened. We don't know why."

"Any sign of an explosive device?"

"Bomb expert confirms no sign of explosives. He was very sure. Something about no explosive smell in the air. We'll keep testing, but right now, an explosive device is way down on the list. The wing appears to have sheared off, not blown off."

Murphy sighed in frustration. "Here's the thing. This is an old plane, and Fiesta is a cheap operator, but you have to work really hard to have the wing fall off your plane like this. I'm not convinced that even they are that bad. Wings just don't fall off of planes. Even a cursory inspection by the pilots before the flight should have revealed a crack big enough to sheer the wing off. We're going to have to put this one back together to really figure out what happened."

With an "Alright, get some rest," Ed cut the team loose for the night.

Jennifer laid awake in the hotel bed. The book was nagging at her. It didn't belong. Sure you could find lots of things that didn't belong in an airplane crash, things like an intact accordion or an unbroken bottle of vodka. Those were normal things that didn't belong. The book wasn't normal. Maybe it was some kind of tourist trinket, but Jennifer didn't think so. She decided that when she got a minute she would check it out.

* * *

Three exhausting weeks later the team had only made progress at eliminating items. They had found most of the pieces from the Fiesta Air 737. Jen had lost weight from spending three days in a hazmat suit in the Texas humidity. The white suits didn't breathe. It was a quick way to lose a few pounds, but it wasn't fun. Jen decided she would stick with running.

The interior of the plane had been horrible. One of the few advantages to the hazmat suit was that the helmet offered a chance to disconnect from reality. Behind the suit's plastic mask Jen could pretend that she was on the moon, or in a very warm video game. The disconnection from reality made it possible to do the job. Of course, once reality intruded back into her brain, she really couldn't throw up in the suit.

Jen would have felt better about her time in the suit if it had led to some answers. Over the last three weeks the NTSB had appropriated an empty hangar at Midland-Odessa airport. Heavy equipment had moved the pieces out of the field and to the hangar. The aircraft was laid out with most of the parts near where they belonged. With the help of a number of volunteer doctors and nurses, they had positively identified all of the remains. It had gone surprisingly quickly. The notification of family members had been much harder. As Murphy had observed, there had been a large number of families and children on the flight. Still, by any measure this had been a text-book crash investigation, except in the one area that mattered, determining the cause of the crash.

The CVR and FDR analysis had come in. The re-corders confirmed the initial suspicions, but didn't provide much in the way of new information. The flight had been boringly normal until the FDR lost all signal from the sensors on the left wing. The pi-lots, unaware that the wing was completely gone, had done everything they could to save the plane. Nothing they could have done would have worked. The recorders did fix the time of the wing separa-tion, but their initial timeline based on the mayday was very close.

They still didn't know why the wing had come off. The engines checked out fine and it was hard to pin the wing falling off on something the flight crew had done. Maintenance had been surprisingly good, better than anyone suspected. Eco-tourism had been good to Fiesta Air and they'd poured some of that money back into maintenance. The crash investiga-tion was stalled. Clearly the problem was structural, but they didn't know why the wing had separated. They were reaching for anything, running down any lead they could find. The worst thing that could happen was for a crash to remain unsolved.

It can take a year for the NTSB to issue a full report with recommendations on a crash the size of Fiesta Air 169. Much of that is documentation, but in most crashes, a preliminary cause is known within a few weeks, especially if the CVR and FDR are found. They had a cause, the wing separated from the fuselage. They didn't have a reason.

Jennifer knew that most crashes were the result of a cascade of events. Poor maintenance leads to a worn part. A worn part breaks during flight. The pilot should be able to compensate, but weather or alcohol or some other factor slows their reaction time leading to a crash. The accident could have been avoided at any point in the sequence. That hadn't happened here. The wing had sheared off. The pilots had no chance.

Jennifer couldn't get the book out of her head. It was time to see if it meant something.

# 3.

I T WAS LATE AFTERNOON WHEN JEN landed in Nashville and rented a car. Despite their small budget, the NTSB was willing to spend a fortune to figure out why a plane crashed. Budgetary concerns were easy to overcome when it came to figuring out what had killed congressional constituents. With the investigation into Fiesta Air 196 stalled, the team was pulling on threads hoping the answer would unravel. Jen was chasing one of those threads.

She had finally shown the book to Ed and the team. They had guessed that book was Aztec or Mayan. While everyone agreed that it was odd, none of them felt Jennifer's passion for it. This was her clue, so she flew to Nashville to meet with one of the country's true experts on Mayan culture.

From the airport Jen went west on Interstate 40. Her iPhone pumped out directions and she turned down Elliston Street looking for Nashville Rare Books.

The neighborhood was in transition from shabby to trendy. Old buildings in various stages of refurbishment marked the landscape. Jen slowed, looking for the address. She drove past it twice. Finally she saw a small metal sign pointing to a stairway. Jen found a spot down the street and parallel parked the rented Nissan. She was dressed casually in jeans, sneakers, and untucked button down shirt. After three weeks she was too tired to dress up.

Jen climbed the stairs to the entrance and noticed a small sign. The store kept some very odd hours. Today it closed at five. She checked her phone, four-thirty, perfect.

A bell rung when Jen opened the door. Despite the windows overlooking the street, the shop was dark, slightly musty smelling, and completely stuffed with old books.

"Hello?" Jen called out. Her voice wavered. She sounded hesitant. Damn it, why was her voice cracking? Jen looked around the store. It was designed to look expensive, even intimidating. Three walls were lined with books. The front wall was dominated by windows overlooking the street below. The windows were heavily tinted and horizontal blinds were turned to ensure that direct sunlight didn't reach the books. The center of the room held an arrangement of furniture. A couch, love seat, and chair formed a semi-circle around a rectangular coffee table. A small desk sat near the door.

Clearly this wasn't your average used paperback store observed Jen. All the volumes on the shelves were leather bound. Several were locked behind glass. There wasn't a Tom Clancy thriller in sight. The nature of the books, the inefficient store layout, odd hours, and the location away from foot traffic told Jen that most of the sales were probably to collectors. The store existed as a vehicle for credibility. Beyond that it was a fancy storage shed.

A man emerged from the back room.

"Dr. Gutierrez?"

The man stuck out his hand.

"That's me," he said. "Please call me Max. Doctor Gutierrez is only for my students."

Dr. Maximilian Gutierrez was not what Jennifer expected. For a rare book store owner, and professor of Mayan studies at Vanderbilt, she'd been expecting someone older, fussier and more...well... Hispanic. The man in front of her certainly didn't fit her stereotype. Not that she was complaining. Dr.

Gutierrez was easier on the eyes than the image of the fussy, old man she had in her head.

When an NTSB researcher spit out his name as a tenured professor of Mayan studies and a rare book expert, she'd pictured a little old man. Sort of a Hispanic Einstein. That was not what she saw in front of her. Jen guessed that Max was in his early thirties, maybe a shade over six feet tall, with round glasses. He's working a graduate professor look in those jeans and sport coat, she thought. He was also very pale, his brown hair tinged with red.

"I'm Jennifer Lynch with the NTSB," she explained. "I called about a book."

"Ah yes, from the plane crash in Texas. I'm not sure what you expect a professor of Mayan studies to do, but I'll help any way that I can."

"Thanks for seeing me. You're not quite what I anticipated. I hope I have the right Dr. Gutierrez."

He smiled. "Well, I'm the Dr. Gutierrez who is a professor of Mayan studies at Vanderbilt. The only thing I like as much as the Maya are books. I managed to combine the two and write four books on Mayan culture." He walked over, reached behind the desk, and pulled out a modern hardback. Jen took it. The back cover showed a black and white glossy of the man standing in front of her.

"It's confusing to my students too. My father was Mexican. That's where both the Gutierrez and the Maximilian come from. He wanted a strong name. My mother was Irish. Between the Spanish name and the light skin I get a lot of double takes."

Relieved that she had the right expert, Jen started again. "I'm following up on something unusual found in the wreckage of Fiesta Air flight 169. It looks like a book and we think it could be Mayan. You were recommended as an expert on both books and the Maya, so here I am."

Max laughed. "It's nice to be wanted again. After the world didn't end in 2012 with the end of the Mayan calendar, we Mayan experts haven't exactly been in high demand."

Jen liked his laugh. He smiled with his eyes and with his cheeks. Slowly Jennifer pulled the book from her bag. It was wrapped in a protective evidence bag. She had signed it out that morning.

Max carefully set the book down on the counter. He pulled a pair of latex gloves from his pocket. Without removing the book from the plastic sleeve, he examined the front. He squinted at it from different angles and turned the book over. Carefully, Max examined the back too. With the gloves on, he slowly removed the book. When he had it halfway out of the cellophane bag he stopped and stared.

Quickly Max slid the book back into the bag. He turned to Jennifer he said, "You know who I am, can I see some identification please." It was not a question.

Jennifer was surprised by both the timing and the tone of the request. Usually, people wanted to see ID up front or they never asked to see it all. It's not like she was FBI or anything. Plus, Max seemed irritated. She pulled out her NTSB identification. Max took it and leaned over an ancient looking computer on the desk. On the PC he found the NTSB's website and clicked until he had a Washington D.C. number. Twenty minutes and three transfers later he confirmed that Jennifer was in fact an NTSB investigator.

After the first transfer, Jennifer took a seat on the chair in the middle of the room and started checking email on her phone. She might be a junior member of the go team, but she had plenty of experience with Washington bureaucracy.

Finally, Max put the phone down. "I'm sorry," Max began, "but is this some kind of joke? Am I being punked?"

Jennifer looked at him quizzically. "Not as far as I know. I personally pulled this book from the aircraft wreckage eight hours after the crash. I don't know what it is, but I can assure you that it was on that plane."

Pointedly ignoring the NTSB agent, Max laid a velvet covered pad onto the open space on his desk. He slid the book from its wrapping and gently placed it on the pad. Frowning, the professor rooted around in his desk for a magnifying glass and leaned in for an even closer look. Slowly, almost reverently he turned the pages, his magnifying glass focused on the edges and corners. Max weighed the book in his hands. He examined the folds, carefully opening and closing several of them.

After a few minutes, Max went back to the ancient PC and started an internet search. Jen watched him click, compare the book to the screen, then click again. Finally Max stood up. He carried the desk pad with the book on it over to the coffee table and set it down gently. "I will need to do more tests, a lot more tests," Max began, "but right now this looks like a Mayan codex from the around the time of the birth of Christ.."

"A Codex?"

"Yes. It's like a book, but one long folded sheet, kind of like an extended pamphlet. A codex is not bound like a book. The thing is, there are only three known Mayan codices in existence. There is a fragment of a fourth, about eleven pages, but the validity of that one is in doubt. None of them are in as good a shape as this one. It's perfect. It shouldn't look this good, even without surviving a plane crash. A real codex would be worn. A Mayan codex uses paper made from the inner bark of a tree, often the wild fig tree. It's called amate paper and some people still make it today in the highlands of Central America. It's organic so it breaks down over time. A real codex wouldn't be this bright unless it had been stored in a properly sealed environment, or it was magic." He winked. "Right now I seriously doubt its authenticity, but it is impressive."

Jen cocked her head. "If it's fake, why is it impressive?" she asked.

"Here's the thing, forgeries all focus on getting the apparent age of the document right. They work really hard to get the paper, the look, and the ink color right. If they screw up, it's in the symbols. This one is the opposite. The symbols are perfect. They are consistent with the Dresden codex, but they seem older, richer. We can spot a fake by testing the age of the document. Unscrupulous collectors usually don't go that far or the forger uses a bogus expert to authenticate the age. This copy is too clean to be real. It's also too clean to be a good forgery. If I were guessing, I would say that it's an incomplete fake. Whoever made this didn't get a chance to fin-ish faking the age. What can you tell me about where you found it?"

Jen described the crash and her experience find-ing the book. When she was done Max looked at her.

"This Codex should never have left Mexico. If it's real, it's a national treasure of the Mexican people," Max said. "If it's fake, all it does is muddy the waters of what we know about the Maya."

"Right now, it's evidence in a crash that killed a hundred and sixty people. If it's real, I'm sure that the United States will be happy to return it to the Mexican people once this crash is solved. So how do we figure out if it's real or not?"

Max slid the codex back into the evidence bag. "First, we order dinner because this is going to take a while."

They ordered from Siam Pad Thai, an upscale Thai place down the block. While they waited, Max made Jennifer repeat the story of finding the Codex in minute detail. He shuddered as she described the carnage, but he tried to focus on where the flight had originated from. Once the food arrived, Max turned the sign on the door to 'closed' and locked the door.

After the Pad Thai was gone, they moved on to the codex. Max leaned back on the couch. "So what do you know about the Maya?"

Jen smiled. "They were Central American, they built pyramids, and in at least one bad movie, the world ended when their calendar ran out."

Max chuckled. "Ok, let's start with the basics and I'll try not to go all snooty professor on you.

The Maya started in Central America in roughly 2000 B.C. Their civilization hit its zenith during the period 250 A.D. to 900 A.D., more or less. They were in decline when the Spanish arrived. The Spaniards finally broke the Maya in the fifteen and sixteen hundreds.

The Maya were unusual in that they had a fully developed system of writing, a calendar, and some amazing art, not to mention kick-ass pyramids that we're still finding in the jungle. They were astronomers and much of their calendar was based on the movement of Venus. Oddly they did all of that without draft animals, without the wheel, and without metal tools. It took lots and lots of manual labor. That led to wars as different cities tried to capture their enemies and boost the availability of slaves. It also leads to speculation today that aliens helped with all of this."

Max's eyes twinkled as Jen laughed at his alien comment. His voice showed his passion for the subject. Jen suspected that he was a very good professor.

"Seriously. Even the Minister of Tourism for the Mexican state of Campeche has claimed alien influence. Plus a 2012 documentary making claims of a Mayan alien connection won an award at the Sundance film festival.

It's all nonsense of course. If you were going to give alien technology to an ancient civilization wouldn't you start with the wheel or metallurgy? Like all civilizations, the Maya eventually started to decline. There are lots of theories as to why. They include drought, war, and disease. What we know for sure is that because there wasn't a single, central Mayan government it was harder for the Spanish to defeat them. This led the Spanish to take an even harder line with the Maya. That hard line included Spanish priests burning Mayan codices, so very few have survived. One example, in 1562 Bishop Diego de Landa ordered all Mayan codices in the Yucatan burned. He thought that conversion would be easier if the Mayan's couldn't fall back on their old religion."

Jen was starting to lose interest.

"Ok, enough history." Max moved on. "Three known codices have survived. They are named for their locations, the Dresden codex is the oldest and in the best shape. It is pre-Columbian, but it's still not much older than the time when the Spanish showed up. There are also the Madrid and Paris codices. The Madrid codex is believed to postdate the Spanish arrival. The Paris codex is in the worst shape. It's been misplaced and rediscovered a number of times over the years.

The Grolier codex is an eleven page fragment of a larger codex. It was supposedly found in a dry cave in 1970. The Grolier is held in a museum in Mexico, but it's not on display. It's also not taken seriously by most scholars. There have been other codices discovered, mostly in tombs, typically as illegible lumps of decomposed material.

Finally, forgeries have been around for more than a hundred years. William Randolph Hearst had two in his collection. The Grolier codex has the right paper, but the symbols are wrong. That's why many think it's a fake.

Jen looked thoughtful. "What would a good forgery be worth?"

Max chewed on that for a moment. "From a few hundred grand to a million maybe. The market for Mayan artifacts is down since the world didn't end. You'd have to fool the right collector to get a million bucks. You'd also have to have an unscrupulous expert. A real expert would spot a fake or insist a genuine codex be turned over to the government. There are three Mayan codices in the world. If another is found, it belongs to the people of Mexico, Belize, or Guatemala, depending on what country it's found in."

"So a good forgery might be worth killing for?"

"Yes, and a bad forgery might be worth killing over when it's discovered. Still, don't you think it's a pretty big jump from murder to mass murder of more than a hundred and fifty people over something that might be worth a million dollars?"

Jen shrugged not yet wanting to accept his logic. "Are there any Maya left? Could someone be trying to get it back?"

Max nodded. "There are plenty of people in Central America who trace their ancestry back to the Mayans. Some still speak the old language and try to keep the Mayan traditions alive. Again, it's a big leap to mass murder. Why don't we take another look at our codex?"

Max and Jennifer cleared the coffee table. Max retrieved the package and again pulled out the codex gingerly with gloved hands. He laid it on a bed of acid free paper on the coffee table to examine it, first with a magnifying glass and then with a microscope.

His iPhone was recording while he described the codex.

"This appears to be a Mayan codex from the late Mayan period, roughly 4 B.C. The folds, colors and the depictions are consistent with what we would expect from that period. The document is roughly equivalent to one hundred pages long," he began.

During a very long night, Max and Jennifer photographed every page of the codex. They unfolded it and measured its full length at a little over twelve feet. Max compared the drawings in the codex with the three known Mayan codices. Each museum had published photos online and that helped with the comparison.

Around eleven they broke out beers, being careful to keep them away from the codex. Finally, at two in the morning, Max collapsed into a chair. Jen sat across him nursing a warm Yazoo Pale Ale. Max looked at her and said, "We have to carbon date the document and the ink. That's the only way to authenticate the age for sure. The problem is that we need a sample to properly date it and I'm not willing carve out a sample on the off chance that it's real."

"So you think it's real?"

"No. I still think it's a very, very good fake," replied Max.

"Why?"

"The condition is just too good. It's perfect. It came through a plane crash unscathed on a plane that it should never have been on. If it's a couple of thousand years old, it's perfectly preserved," Max finished.

"But," Jen let that hang.

"Yeah, I know. It's flawless. It reads like the other codices, but it's more complete. It would take a genius to fake this. I sure as hell couldn't." Max finished.

"So what's your theory? What is this thing?"

Max thought a moment. "At first I thought it was a forgery for the tourists, like a Caribbean treasure map, but it's too good. I still think it might be a good forgery that wasn't complete yet. Like fake bills that haven't yet been marked yet with blue and red fibers. Maybe it's a proof, showing someone that it could be done. That's really the best theory I have. The Mayan equivalent of faking a Renoir."

Jen looked at him. "Can you read it?"

Max gently opened the codex. "It's the book of Q'uq'umatz, the Mayan sky god. He is represented as a feathered serpent and a co-creator of the world along with the god Tepeu. Q'uq'umatz has similarities to the Aztec god Quetzalcoatl, though their stories diverge widely. It is believed that there were codices for other Mayan gods so this is at least consistent."

Jennifer got up and leaned over his shoulder as he stared at the pictographs in the codex. She smelled like Thai spices, beer, and a long day. Max liked that smell on her. He was glad that she had moved closer. His gloved fingers carefully flipped the pages.

"The book tells the story of the creation of the world. It defines the priesthood and the sacrifices that Q'uq'umatz requires. It includes prayers for rain, for harvest and fertility. It also brutally describes the treatment of prisoners."

As Max moved through the book, Jennifer realized that she could understand the pictographs. It was almost as if she could read the codex. Slowly she started to read ahead of Max silently. This shouldn't be possible she realized.

Near the middle, Max started to quote a curse in the center of the book. "He who disturbs the book of Q'uq'umatz..."

"...shall suffer death from above," finished Jennifer.

Max was angry now. "How did you know that? How could you know that?"

Jennifer stood there stunned. The words had just come out. "I can read the Codex," she said. "I don't know how or why but I can read it."

"Do you know how long it took me to understand how to read Mayan glyphs?" Max began.

Jennifer cut him off. "Look, I'm sure it was a long time, but I can read this." Now she was upset. They glared at each other. Finally, Jennifer stepped back. Calmer, quieter, she said, "Look, we're both exhausted. You go home. I'll go to my hotel and we can figure this out in the morning."

Max looked hurt, but he drew himself up and said, "Ok. I have a safe in back for really rare documents. Do you want to keep this in there overnight?"

"No, I have to keep the codex with me. It may be evidence of something. Can we meet in the morning? Something weird is going on here and I'm running out of time to figure out why a hundred and sixty people died."

Max agreed. "I can hand tomorrow's class off to a grad student. The shop is technically closed until three. I'll be here around nine."

Jennifer found her hotel in the dark and crashed into bed without undressing. The next morning she hadn't gotten enough sleep, but coffee and eggs had done wonders. The thought that they could have a motive behind the crash didn't hurt either. She showed up at Max's shop a little after nine. He had brought pastries and Jennifer grabbed a bear claw.

To get started, Max dragged an ancient looking chalkboard on a wheeled stand from somewhere in the back. "I thought we could start listing what we know," he said.

Jen started ticking items off while Max wrote. Each time she held up a finger to indicate an item, she licked off a little bear claw icing. "We have a crashed plane with a hundred and sixty dead. We have a possible ancient codex of a Mayan sky god, in perfect condition, and apparently mortals can read it. It might also be fake."

Max started a new column. He said, "If this is real it's priceless. Even a fake could lead someone to kill. Could there have been a collector or treasure hunter on the plane?" He added these thoughts to the board.

Jen checked her notes on passengers from the crash. "No one stood out, but we can go back through the passenger manifest with that in mind."

"We have to get the codex tested. Determining whether or not it's real may make a huge difference. We need the age of the paper and the ink via radio carbon dating."

"I'll try to get permission for testing." As she finished her pager went off. Jen went white. "I have to go. Another plane has gone down. I'll call you when I know more." Jen grabbed the codex, along with the rest of her stuff and ran out the door.

# 4.

THREE HOURS EARLIER EMILY ADAMS was waiting for her flight from Des Moines to Atlanta on Triangle Air. Her parents had divorced eight years ago and her dad fled to Atlanta for a better job. Emily endured years of flight attendants escorting her on visits to see him. Now, as a sixteen year old, she could make the trip without feeling like a child. Emily wasn't looking forward to this trip. The divorce had been hard on her. As she moved into high school her grades slipped, her friends changed, and she'd been caught experimenting with pot. Emily had learned to tune out her mom's parental rants, but now she would have to deal with her dad's approach.

The Des Moines school system still hadn't discovered that Emily was a visual learner. This explained some of the slip in her grades. It also explained her secret love of comic books. It took her months to read a short book for English class but only three days to tear through the nine hundred plus pages of *The Walking Dead, Compendium One.*

At the airport Emily used her new found freedom to browse the meager shops at the gate. When she was younger they had seemed huge; filled with exotic candy and strange magazines. Now they seemed like sad little reminders of the mall she spent so much time at. The reading section was filled with nothing but fashion magazines and paperbacks. Not a comic book in sight.

She turned to leave when a book caught her eye. It was a comic book, sort of. Emily picked up the strange book. It was folded, not bound. The pictures were crude but somehow intriguing. There were no words, but as she browsed through it, she realized that she understood the drawings. This book was special. She had to have it. Emily flipped the book over. Odd, there was no bar code, no price, and no publisher. Not even a title.

She thought about just putting the book in her backpack, but she really didn't want to get arrested at the airport. The one time she had been caught shoplifting at the mall had been awful. Do they have airport jail? Emily shook off the random thoughts and brought the book to the counter. The tired looking woman behind the register tried to scan it. She tried to find a price or a bar code without success. A line was forming behind Emily. People trying to buy water, mints and magazines for their upcoming flights were getting restless. Emily's cheeks reddened as the line got longer. Finally, the lady behind the counter put the book in a bag. She leaned forward and whispered, "Just take it. If it's not in the system, it can't be stealing."

Emily shoved the book in her backpack. It sucks when it's harder to buy a book than to steal it, she thought. Emily wandered back to her gate and found her flight ready to board. Onboard, she sat back in her seat. The placard in the seat back pocket said that this was an Airbus A320. Whatever, after a while, all planes start to look the same. Once they were airborne, Emily remembered her book.

Emily cruised through the comic book. This wasn't the sort of comic that she normally read, but the story of the sky god of the Maya fascinated her. Midway through she found a curse on those who would disturb Q'uq'umatz. "Death from above," was how she interpreted the curse. As she mouthed the saying, she shivered. Her second feeling wasn't a shiver, it was a shudder as both wings separated from the plane and scattered debris over southern Illinois.

* * *

In Nashville, Jennifer wasn't that far away. She could drive to the crash site faster than she could fly so she pushed the rented Nissan hard and headed northwest on I-24.

Like the first crash, the plane had gone down in field in the middle of nowhere. The debris was scattered across the Missouri/Illinois line, south of St. Louis. Five hours later, Jennifer managed to be the first NTSB responder on the scene. She took charge directing police and firefighters to secure the sight.

Normally an NTSB investigator wouldn't work two crashes at a time. Then again, it had been a long time since there were two crashes this close together. Jennifer tried to remember the last time there had been multiple crashes of this magnitude in the same year. Nothing came to mind. Certainly nothing from the modern era of jet travel. Jennifer knew that she wouldn't be assigned to this crash full time so her focus was on establishing a perimeter and securing the scene for the ultimate team.

It was clear from the debris field that the plane had come apart in the sky. Aircraft and body parts were scattered across a wide arc. It appeared as though the wings had not just come off, but had ripped the fuselage apart during separation. Flags arrived from Lambert-St. Louis International Airport and Jennifer bent down to mark a severed torso. It would be the first in a very long night of marking body parts. They gloss over this part in the interview process, she thought.

It would take five very long days just to find all the bodies. Jennifer's quick arrival had helped secure the scene and the assigned Go Team was grateful. A week after Jennifer had driven like a maniac into a field of horrors, she finished reviewing the crash with the team that would ultimately work this mess. Jennifer confessed that the Texas crash was no closer to being solved, and this one had some eerie similarities. The debris that they had recovered so far was being tagged and assembled in a hangar across the state line in Missouri. St Louis had the best facility that they could find.

Exhausted, Jennifer walked slowly through the hangar. She found herself in the section where they were sorting, tagging, and cataloging passenger items. The sheer amount of detritus that was not a physical part of the airplane or a passenger was incredible. Absentmindedly, she looked down at a table and stared. She knew that book. It was the Mayan codex.

"Where did you find this?" Jennifer was almost yelling as she grabbed one of the volunteers. Her eyes were wild with excitement and lack of sleep. The volunteer took a step back and used a calm, soothing voice with the crazy woman holding the book. "Grid 37," was the reply. "We found it just like that. It's remarkably clean, not a mark on it. The separation of both wings meant that there wasn't much fuel left to ignite when the fuselage pancaked in. Most of the passenger's personal electronics didn't survive the fall, but the paper items did."

Still clutching the codex, Jennifer rushed to find her backpack. "Hey, you can't take that. That's evidence," the volunteer yelled after her. Jennifer found her backpack in a corner near the personnel entrance. The volunteer followed, still yelling. A few of the NTSB team members walked over to see what was going on. As the team leader, walked up, Jennifer yelled, "Yes!" and pulled out the copy of the codex from the first crash. It was still encased in the protective plastic envelope with the chain of evidence log attached.

Jennifer held the two up for the group. "It's a link," she exclaimed. Their faces looked dubious. Richard Crownover, the investigator in charge for this crash, pushed his way to the front of the little crowd. "It's a book," he said. "I'm sure we'll find any number of best sellers in common between the crashes. After all, most airport bookstores all sell the same stuff." His look said that Jennifer had been working too hard on these crashes.

Jennifer shook her head. "This isn't a normal book. It's a Mayan codex. I just had this one examined by an expert in Nashville. That's why I was close to this crash. I was there when I got the call. The expert was trying to figure out if the codex is real or a fake. Look, even if it's a fake, what are the chances of two fake Mayan codices being involved in crashes where the airplane comes apart?"

Crownover looked thoughtful. "Two Mayan codices on two crashes is crazy of course. Hell, two crashes this close together where the plane comes apart is crazy," he added. "Clearly it's not the cause of the crash, but it could be a signature. Still, it's the most bizarre signature I've ever heard of."

He shook his head. "I thought we were done worrying about the Mayans when the world didn't end in 2012. Frankly, I'm more worried that we have two planes from two different manufacturers where the wings are falling off. If it was one model of plane or even planes from a single manufacturer we could ground them all and inspect them. We'd catch hell over the cost, but it could be done and done fairly quickly. There's no sign of a bomb so far which means we could end up recommending that the entire U.S. aircraft fleet be inspected. That won't go over well with anyone."

Richard turned to Jennifer and said, "Drag your expert up here. This may be a wild goose chase, but it's odd enough to be a link. Let him examine both books. I've got phone calls to make."

Jennifer had calls to make too. First up was Max who was stunned to hear that there was another codex. "It can't be original if there is more than one," he commented, but he agreed to drive up and examine the document. She called Ed Rollins and updated him. She had called him on the drive up a week ago to tell him what she had learned about the first manuscript. Now they had a very tentative link between the crashes. Ed was skeptical too but he agreed that the lead was worth pursuing. It was, after all, the only lead they had.

Jennifer went to the team hotel and slept while Max made the five hour plus drive from Nashville to St. Louis. When Jennifer returned to the hangar six hours later, Max was carefully examining the second codex. Jennifer had yet to let the first codex out of her sight.

Max didn't look up as Jennifer approached. "If I didn't know better, I'd swear that this was the same codex I examined last week. There can't be two per-fect copies. One or both of these has to be a fake."

"And hello to you to," Jennifer began. Max looked up. "You look like hell," he said with a smile.

"No," she replied with a grin. "Hell was six hours ago, before a shower and a nap. You should have seen me then."

With that, Jennifer pulled out the codex from the Texas crash. Max laid them side by side, each on their own protective envelope. He was already wear-ing gloves and he picked up a magnifying glass. He seems more like Dr. Watson than Sherlock Holmes was Jen's random thought. Where did that come from?

Max went through each page, methodically com-paring both manuscripts, first with a magnifying glass and then with a jeweler's loop. After more than an hour he finally stepped back from the table and sighed. "They are a perfect match," he declared. "Too perfect."

A small crowd gathered around the table. "What the hell is that supposed to mean?" asked a suddenly tired Jennifer.

"Look, when you examine two documents this closely there are always some anomalies. Handwrit-ten documents have different pen strokes, squiggles, and goofs. Copiers leave smudges and minute roller marks. Paper moves unevenly through printers and pages dry differently leaving small differences. Even professionally printed material leaves some tiny variation. These aren't copies. They are more like exact clones."

Max turned to Jennifer. "We have to get the paper and ink tested. That's the only way to know for sure how old these are."

# 5.

FLYING FROM SAN FRANCISCO TO New York, Mario was bored. He had sold his startup software business three months ago for twenty million dollars. It wasn't enough to buy his own jet, but the first class seat on the AmerAir 767 was still pretty comfortable. In spite of that, Mario was restless.

After selling his firm, he had tried to learn golf, then guitar and finally sailing, all unsuccessfully. All he really knew how to do was code, and that's what he loved. Now he was on his way to talk to the New York based partners of a venture capital firm. He'd already made a good impression on the California partners, but New York wanted to meet him before they invested in his new idea. His restlessness wasn't nerves; he was just ready to start something new.

Mario pulled out his iPad and connected to the plane's Wi-Fi. He opened his e-eader intending to start a new biography of Steve Jobs. That's when he saw the odd, untitled book cover. He certainly hadn't downloaded that. He didn't think you could have an untitled eBook. Curious, Mario opened it. There were no words, only pictures. Not pictures in a graphic novel sense like *Injustice, Gods Among Us*. Mario was a nerd after all and no stranger to comic books. This book had pictures like pyramid paintings or cave glyphs. The drawings were beautifully rendered. As he stared at them, he found that with a little time and effort, he could understand the pictures.

While the other passengers in first class slept or worked on their laptops, Mario read or rather, watched. He wasn't sure what you called reading pictures. Midway through he came to a passage that he interpreted as a curse on those who would steal the book of Q'uq'umatz. As he read that passage, a wrenching sound of tearing metal filled his ears. He watch horrified as the front of the fuselage peeled open like a can of tuna. Passengers screamed as laptops, briefcases and flight attendants were sucked into the void.

The void sucked at Mario trying to pull him from his seat, but his seatbelt held. Still, he slammed his head against the seat in front of him. The iPad disappeared into the sky as the entire cockpit, with the pilot and first officer still strapped into their seats, peeled away from the rest of the plane, and fell. That can't happen Mario's brain screamed as his mind fought against the fear of death. Mercifully, the loss of pressure at altitude caused most of the passengers to pass out.

With a loss of control, the plane plummeted thirty-eight thousand feet onto the South Dakota plain.

\* \* \*

In St. Louis, Jennifer was on the phone with Ed Rollins working out how to get the codices carbon dated. She was planning on delivering them personally to a lab once they had a plan. Ed excused himself and put her on hold. He was eerily calm when he came back on the line. "Jen, there's been another crash." Jennifer drew a deep breath as Ed continued. "We don't know anything yet, but we're rolling our last go team. If we have another crash we're either going to have to pull the team that worked the Texas Fiesta Air crash or ask the military for help. We're just not prepared for this many crashes in a short period of time."

"Ed, make sure they look for a codex."

Without fanfare, Ed hung up to go deal with another crash. Jennifer had been working too hard. She'd spent way too much time working crashes over the last month. To try to feel normal again she headed down to the hotel lobby. The bar was about half full and a number of the Illinois crash team members were there. She took an empty seat with them and ordered white wine. Everyone was watching the TV above the bar.

The second crash in less than a month had kept the news outlets busy. Reporters had crawled over west Texas and southern Illinois looking for an angle. There had been feature and human interest stories. Now the third and newest crash was the only news story of the day. The media was gleefully fostering unrestrained panic. While Fiesta Air was a third rate airline with suspicious maintenance practices, Triangle and AmerAir were mainline carriers. That had the public running scared. Retired engineers from Boeing and Airbus tried to provide a counterpoint to the chaos, but reason rarely prevails amid group panic.

"Is there anything new on the South Dakota crash?" Jennifer asked no one in particular. She was focused on the TV. Two seats down a balding man in his fifties that Jen recognized as a structural engineer spoke up.

"One of the Boeing guys called me," he said. "The cockpit peeled apart from the rest of the fuselage at the forward doors. Not like Aloha 243 where the roof peeled off like a sardine can. It tore around," he twirled his finger in a circle sideways and repeated the word for emphasis, "around like a soup can in a can opener. That can't happen. The physics don't work. The slipstream should have peeled the roof back if it separated." The engineer stared hard at her and then looked dejectedly at his beer.

Jennifer knew that in 1988, Aloha flight 243 had suffered explosive decompression in flight when the roof of the cabin peeled away just behind the forward doors. Flight attendant C.B. Lansing had been sucked out of the plane, the only fatality in an accident that could have been much, much worse. She also knew that engineers from the manufactures routinely worked with the NTSB on crash investigations. No one knew the inner workings of an airplane like its manufacturer. If the Boeing guys were freaked out about this, things were about to get very bad.

\* \* \*

Three days later Jennifer was in Washington D.C. Since the NTSB didn't normally have to worry about authenticating the age of documents, the director had called in a favor. The Smithsonian had provided the name of a lab in Virginia that they used for dating documents. The lab was experienced with providing expert testimony on document provenance. This was important. If the crashes turned out to be terrorist events, the lab could maintain the chain of evidence for trial.

Jennifer was headed there now. She was reluctant to let the codices out of her sight at this point. This was their only lead and it was a crazy lead. She was met in the lobby by a Dr. Mueller and shown back to his office. "It's nice to meet you Ms. Lynch. We don't often get called in to help out the NTSB so this should be interesting. I was afraid that today would be boring," began the doctor.

"Please, call me Jennifer. Thank you for seeing me today doctor. You've heard about the recent crashes I assume?" Mueller nodded.

"We've found an unusual document at two of the crash sites and we are trying to understand if the documents are related to the crash. An expert we've consulted, believes that the first document is a Mayan forgery. He is less sure now that the second document has surfaced. Two perfect forgeries is only slightly less likely than two perfect originals. We would like to have the documents carbon dated, along with any other tests that might help us determine their age and authenticity."

Mueller leaned back in his chair and pressed his hands into a pyramid. He paused before responding. "Before you show me the documents, I have a few questions, if that's alright? You say documents, could you be more specific?" he asked.

"They appear to be Mayan codices," answered Jen. She assumed an expert on documents wouldn't need an explanation of what a codex was.

"Who is your expert and why does he think they are forgeries?" continued the doctor.

"Max Gutierrez. He's a professor of Mayan studies at Vanderbilt. He was impressed by the documents. He said that the Mayan symbols and subject matter seem perfect, but the codex is in really good shape...near perfect shape," Jennifer explained. "Too good to have been in a cave for thousands of years. That was bad enough. When a second copy was found, Max, that is, Dr. Gutierrez, was convinced that both were fake."

"I am familiar with Dr. Gutierrez. He has been helpful with identifying counterfeit Mayan objects that unscrupulous dealers have tried to sell to various museums. This should be much more interesting than a day full of meetings. May I see the codices now please?"

Jennifer slid the carefully wrapped codices from their protective packages. Mueller pulled on a pair of latex gloves.

"Magnificent" was his comment when he removed the first codex. Jennifer spoke up. "Dr. Gutierrez, confirmed that the two documents are identical so we are being very careful to ensure that the two are not mixed up. It may be important later to understand which codex is associated with which crash."

"I understand. We will need to do some chemical testing on the documents in addition to carbon dating. As I'm sure that Dr. Gutierrez mentioned, all of the known Mayan codices have been printed on paper known as amate, made from inner tree bark. That alone goes a long way toward identifying fakes. We will do our best to ensure that the testing has a minimum impact on both documents. The tests will take a couple of hours to perform, but finalizing the results will require a few days. We can perform the tests and return the codices today. I assume that you want to wait for them?"

"Absolutely," Jennifer replied. "Given the sensitive nature of these crashes, we are quite protective of anything that might be helpful to us."

"Would you like to watch?"

Relieved that the Codices would still be in sight, Jennifer agreed. With that, Mueller returned the Codex to its envelope. He led Jennifer to a lab down the hall.

* * *

Happy to be back in her own bed in Atlanta, Jennifer ran a mere two miles the next morning. The last several months had seen too many late nights and junk food, paired with too little exercise. The exercise felt good and it hurt. As she walked into her apartment, her cell phone rang.

"Jen," she answered.

"Hi Jennifer. I'm Marcia Ghent and I'm an NTSB technician working the AmerAir South Dakota crash site. Ed Rollins asked me to call you directly."

Jen felt her gut tighten. "Did you find a strange book in the crash?" she asked.

"Well, not really," she began. "But what we did find was pretty strange. Understand, this plane did a free fall from thirty-eight thousand feet with one end of the fuselage completely open to the atmosphere. Everything not bolted or nailed down got sucked out of that plane as it tumbled and fell."

The Boeing engineer was right about that part, thought Jen. She put Marcia on speaker and took off her shoes. Jen peeled off her shorts to get ready for a shower.

Marcia continued, "The debris was scattered over miles. We're still finding things. But one of the things we found was an iPad. Normally they are as fragile as a dozen eggs, but somehow this one survived a thirty-eight thousand foot free fall and still works. When we turned it on, it opened up to an eBook that looks an awful lot like the book you asked us to look out for. I've emailed you a copy."

Jennifer stopped with her shirt halfway over her head. Did she hear that right? "Marcia, can you say that again?"

"The iPad works, your magic book was on it, and I've emailed you a copy."

Jennifer ran to her bag and pulled out her own iPad. She opened her email, and there she saw the codex, staring back at her big as life. She was still sweaty from her run and she was barely dressed, but none of that mattered as she slowly settled into a chair staring at the screen.

"Hello? Are you still there?"

Jen thought a second. "Is it possible that some-one got to the site early and planted it?"

"Anything is possible, but we went through the iPad and matched it to a passenger on the manifest. It belonged to a Mario Banelli and it's got his sched-ule, contacts, pictures of his kids, and a couple of movies on it. He was headed to New York for some kind of meeting with investors. If someone planted this after the fact, they did a damn good job."

"Investors huh? I wonder what kind of investors," Jen thought out loud.

"Software investors. It's all over the web. He was some kind of big shot Seattle software entrepreneur drumming up investors for his next genius idea. The nerds are in mourning all over Twitter."

"Thanks Marcia." Jennifer heard herself say. "That was not at all what I was expecting, but now we have the codex at all three crash scenes. Well, sort of the codex, but this is too big of a coinci-dence."

# 6.

FROM BEHIND HIS DESK, THE PRESIDENT of the United States gestured toward the director of the NTSB. "So we have nothing on these crashes?"

In the Oval Office, the director squirmed uncomfortably.

"Mr. President, these crashes have all been the result of massive structural failures," the director said. "Nothing points to a bomb. No explosive residue has been found at any of the scenes, and the debris patterns don't fit an explosive device. At the same time, these are not typical crashes. Wings don't fall off of commercial aircraft in flight. Cockpits don't peel off and fall from the sky. Something is definitely wrong here. Three crashes this close to-gether is stretching the resources of the NTSB. We've got people working around the clock to figure out what is going on. The manufacturers and air-lines are giving us everything they've got too. Eve-ryone involved has a significant financial interest in preventing more incidents."

The President's chief of staff spoke up. "Director, we appreciate all the hard work that your people are doing, but if we can't keep planes from falling from the sky, the entire airline industry is in jeopardy, and by extension, the entire U.S. economy. Surely you remember the mess we had after 9/11?"

The director looked at the President and nodded. "Nobody understands that better than I do Mr. Pres-ident. We have a number of anomalies that we're looking at. In two of the crashes the wings separated. We're working to determine if that's significant. In addition, all of the incidents happened at altitude. Most issues occur during takeoff and landing, so we're looking hard at that. Finally, in two of the crashes, our investigators found some kind of Ma-yan book. We have experts looking at it and they've termed it a codex. The third crash had an electronic version of the codex on an iPad. We're still running tests and digging for leads on this codex, but the chances of such an obscure book showing up at all three scenes is astronomical. It cannot be a coincidence."

"Could it be a terrorist signature?" the President asked.

His chief of staff added to the theory. "Maybe Mexican drug lords sending a message? The President's border control policies have been having a positive effect on the war on drugs. The Mayan angle certainly doesn't sound like a middle eastern group."

"We just don't know yet Mr. President. If these are terrorist acts we don't know how they are bringing the planes down. Other than the books, we have nothing to confirm that the crashes are even connected. We know that this is a priority and we're doing everything we can."

After the Director left, the President turned to his Chief of Staff. "We're getting nowhere. Keep the NTSB involved for their experts, but turn this one over to the FBI."

Looking uncomfortable, the Chief of Staff replied, "Mr. President, we're trying to avoid a panic. Legally, the FBI isn't supposed to take charge until there is evidence of a crime. I'm worried that giving the FBI the lead will imply that we know that this is a terrorist attack and cause a panic. Why don't we invite the FBI to consult? That way if we do have to give the FBI the lead they are already in place."

Grudgingly the President agreed, for now.

* * *

Linda Welsh was a seeker. In her forty years she had worked her way through infatuations with New Age, Wicca, and Kabbalah among other religions. She had even spent some time with Zoroastrianism. Finally she decided to simply describe herself as 'spiritual'. Linda was in Austin for a conference and craft fair that had wrapped up yesterday. She loved Austin. With its Keep Austin Weird slogan, it was more open to new ideas than the rest of Texas. Now the conference was over and it was time to go home to her beloved Boulder, Colorado.

Linda may have been a seeker, but she wasn't a vegetarian. She loved Salt Lick's pulled pork tacos available in the Austin-Bergstrom International Airport. Linda bought two and waited for her Unified Airlines flight. There was something about the sweet heat of those tacos that she found herself craving when she visited Austin. Just one more, she thought. No, I need to watch my weight. Maybe I'll take a walk.

Linda wandered into the bookstore next to the food vendors. A pyramid-like book display caught her eye. Aztec she thought, no Mayan. She walked closer. Linda had spent almost a year studying the Maya well in advance of the 2012 calendar controversy. The Maya were renowned for their knowledge of astronomy and their extensive calendar. The end of the Mayan calendar in December 2012 had prompted many to predict the end of the world. There were a lot of disappointed prophets when the world didn't end.

Linda picked up the book and flipped through it. This was a brilliant reproduction of a Mayan codex. She had to have it. The sign next to the books said that they were free. That couldn't be right. Linda turned to the woman by the register, "Are these really free?" she asked.

"If that's what the sign says," replied by the distracted clerk with a shrug. Linda put a copy in her bag and picked up an extra for her partner back in Boulder. Feeling slightly giddy, she walked down to her gate and boarded her flight to Denver.

After three disastrous crashes, passenger volume was off thirty percent and headed down. Those already holding tickets would probably complete their trips. Business people would still travel come hell or fiery death. If they didn't travel, they couldn't do the deals that got them paid. Everyone else was holding back, waiting to see what was next.

Airlines ostensibly try to make money. To compensate for the recent drop in passenger volume, they had reduced capacity. They accomplished this by flying smaller planes on some routes and new, more fuel efficient planes when they couldn't go smaller. This meant that Linda was flying Unified Air on a small, 50 seat regional jet built by Embraer. Her window seat was behind the single exit row on the right, with a view of the wing.

While taxiing, Linda remembered her new book and pulled it from her bag. She flipped through it. Linda was more of a skimmer than a reader. She felt the plane lift off as she turned pages. Linda stumbled onto the page with the curse and flipped passed it. She heard the plane make a loud rumble. Linda snapped the book shut and looked out the window. Normally she wasn't a nervous flyer, but the recent crashes seemed like an evil omen to her. Her stomach lurched in fear. The plane smoothed out. "Is that a crack in the wing or just a seam?" she wondered idly as she looked out the window.

She opened the middle of the book again and heard a bang. Smoke trailed from the right engine and the plane yawed left with reduced power from the right engine. With the book closed on her lap, the engine smoothed out. No. It can't be, she thought.

After the plane was again smooth and level, Linda opened the book one more time to the middle of the codex. She looked at the pictures very slowly. Linda carefully examined each picture and frequently cut her eyes over to the engine. She flipped to the page with the curse and started to read. She saw the engine catch fire out of the corner of her eye. Linda screamed and slammed the book shut. The engine stayed on fire.

"Mayday, Mayday," the pilot calmly called out over his radio from the cockpit. "This is Unified Air 3675 requesting an emergency return to AUS. Our right engine is on fire." The co-pilot pulled the fire extinguisher handle for the right engine and then started calling out items on the emergency landing checklist.

In the cabin, the flight attendant was fighting panic. She shouted at the passengers, forgetting that there was a public address system. "Please fasten your safety belts, place your head between your legs, and hug your knees."

"And kiss your ass goodbye," the passenger in seat 1B muttered loudly. In seat 9D Linda stuffed the book back into her bag and tried to hug her knees, not an easy movement in the cramped regional jet cabin. She prayed. It was a strange feeling because she wasn't sure who she was praying to, but she wanted more time to find out. She decided to just work her way down the list of religions she had studied.

Fire trucks screamed down the taxiway as Unified Air 3675 floated over the runway, smoke trailing from the right engine. With a screech of tires the captain put the Embraer down on the runway. He let it roll long using only the brakes, not the thrust reversers. He didn't want to deploy the reversers on only one engine. Fire trucks hosed the plane down the whole way.

Inside the aircraft, the flight attendant opened the cabin door dropping the steps on the little jet. She shouted for passengers to only use the left side window exit. In seat 8A, an overweight software salesman pulled down the emergency handle, hefted the fifty pound door, and tossed it out of the window. He was surprisingly agile for a man carrying forty extra pounds. The salesman jumped onto the wing and stayed there helping passengers out, even as the fire trucks rained down water and foam.

The flight attendant told everyone to leave their carry-on luggage. No one listened. Linda crossed the aisle, bag in hand, and went out the opposite window and down the wing. The regional jet was small enough to not need emergency slides. A firefighter caught her as she slid down the wing and roughly handed her off to other emergency personnel who were ushering passengers away from the plane.

Eventually, a bus took all forty eight passengers and three crew to a roped off section of the terminal. It is also the NTSB's responsibility to investigate airborne incidents that don't result in a crash, but it would take them a while to get here. Since the FBI was assisting in the other investigations, they sent over a couple of agents from the nearest FBI field office in San Antonio to interview the passengers. NTSB investigators would go over the plane once they arrived.

One of the passengers suffered a panic attack after safely arriving at the terminal and was hospitalized. The rest of the passengers were released several hours later. It had taken ten minutes for Linda to stop shaking. As the adrenaline subsided, she found that she was exhausted. Amazingly, several passengers left on the next available flight. Linda was not one of those. She was to going need a day or two before she was ready to get on another plane.

Linda didn't tell the FBI about the book. She was afraid that they would think that she was nuts, but she knew what had happened. In her tired state, all she wanted was a hotel room for the night. That left her completely unprepared for the media onslaught that overtook her when she left the terminal.

* * *

Jennifer Lynch was sitting in a Nashville bar with Max Gutierrez. The codex was the only lead they had. None of the nut job groups that had tried to claim credit for the crashes had panned out. They were expecting the results of the radio carbon dating any time now and Jennifer wanted to be near Max when the results came in. To her surprise, she found that she liked being around him.

The TV above the bar was showing news from the close call in Austin. Jennifer was glad to see that there were no fatalities. She had almost caught up on her sleep and she wasn't ready for more faces of the dead to intrude on her dreams. The reporter shoved a microphone in the face of a survivor as she exited the airport.

"Hey, turn it up," Jennifer said to the bartender.

The on screen text identified the passenger as Linda Welsh. As the bartender turned up the sound, it caught Linda in mid-sentence. "...every time I read from the book, the engine would act up, but when I shut the book, the plane flew fine. By the time I fig-ured out what was happening, it was too late. This book is what caused the crash." She held up a Mayan codex.

"Son of a bitch!" Jennifer was on her feet shouting at the TV.

The reporter turned to face the camera with a chuckle. "Well, there you have it. One survivor's theory about what happened on Unified Air flight 3675. We think that NTSB might find a different cause when their investigation is done, but we're glad that, unlike other recent crashes, everyone survived this one. Now back to you Bert." The reporter's tone dripped with sarcasm. Jennifer missed it all. She dropped cash on the bar to cover their drinks and pulled her cell phone out of her jeans as she ran outside. She had Ed Rollins on the phone in under a minute.

"Ed, Austin, Unified Air Flight 3675. We just saw one of the survivors on TV holding up a codex. This could be a huge break. We have a chance to find out where it came from," Jennifer said.

Ed was used to these short conversations and he understood the urgency. "I'll get the FBI to find her and hold her."

"We're on the next plane to Austin," said Jennifer.

"We?" Ed replied.

"I'm here with Max, uh, Dr. Gutierrez. We'll need him to authenticate the codex."

On the other end of the phone, Ed suppressed the knowing smirk in his voice. He'd worked enough crashes to know that the pressure and close working conditions of crash investigations sometimes led to romantic results. Often the endings to these relationships weren't much prettier than the crashes themselves.

"Get there as fast as you can," was all he said.

# 7.

THE CLOSEST FBI OFFICE TO AUSTIN IS in San Antonio, on University Heights Boulevard, just off of I-10. It had taken the FBI three hours to find Linda's hotel. She had been asleep for about an hour when the FBI knocked on her door. To say that she was pissed off was an understatement. The hour and a half drive to the San Antonio field office had not softened her mood.

Early the next morning, an FBI special agent introduced himself as Roberto Torres and led Jennifer and Max to an FBI conference room in the San Antonio field office. There they found Linda, head down on the table, snoring lightly. "Have you talked to her?" Linda asked the agent.

"We didn't even know what to ask," replied the agent. "We were told to pick her up as a material witness in these plane crashes and to hold her until someone from the NTSB got here. We got her name and details of course, but we really don't have anything to hold her on. I hope you guys have something. She did just survive a plane crash, you know."

As they entered the conference room, Linda woke up with a start. Jennifer decided to try a good cop routine. "We are sorry for dragging you down here Ms. Welsh. I'm Jennifer Lynch with the National Transportation Safety Board." She showed her NTSB credentials. Linda squinted at them through tired eyes." This is Dr. Gutierrez. He is working with us on these incidents. We have some questions for you that really can't wait. Can we get you some coffee or something else before we get started?"

Linda rubbed her eyes. "I would love some tea and please, call me Linda," she said. "What is this all about? My plane didn't actually crash."

"We saw your interview on TV and we're interested in the book you were holding," said Jennifer.

"Oh that. I was exhausted and a little overwrought. I'm not quite sure what I even said."

"Tell us anyway. If possible, we would like you to start with where you got the book."

"Do I need a lawyer?"

The agent returned with tea just as Linda uttered these words. He spoke up. "Ms. Welsh, it is of course your right to have a lawyer present. If that is your wish we will suspend any questioning until you've found a lawyer here in San Antonio. However, you are not under arrest, and at this point, you aren't suspected of anything."

The agent looked at Jennifer for confirmation. She nodded her head to indicate that he was correct. This hippy wannabe wasn't yet a suspect.

The agent continued, "It has been my experience that the longer you are here, the more likely it is that the media will find out that we have questions for you. We will only confirm that we consider you to be a potential material witness at this point. Unfortunately, the media has a nasty tendency to make things up when they don't have answers. Is there an attorney that we can call for you?"

Jennifer was impressed. This isn't agent Torres's first rodeo, she thought.

"No, I'm actually from Boulder. I was in Austin for a conference and I'm just trying to get home. Look, I'll answer questions for now. You wanted to know about the book, right? I bought it in one of the airport book stores. Well, I didn't actually buy it. There was a display offering them for free so I took two. One for me and one for my partner back in Boulder. We love anything Mayan."

Jennifer leaned in and asked, "Which bookstore exactly?"

"The one in the center atrium, past security, near the food court." Linda launched into a monologue about tacos, salt lick, and weight loss that Max and Jen barely followed. Finally she described how and where she had found the book. Special Agent Torres had another FBI agent retrieve a map of the airport and Linda pointed out the exact store.

Max spoke up. "May I see the books?"

An FBI agent brought her bag from another room. Linda pulled out two books and set them on the table. They appeared identical to the codices they already had. Max pulled latex gloves from his sport coat and moved to the far end of the long conference table to examine the newest codices.

Jen then walked Linda through the whole ordeal again from her trip to the airport through the FBI visit. Max looked like his attention was focused on the codices, but when Linda finished he spoke up. "Linda, is it okay if we take your fingerprints? I would like to be able to exclude them from any other prints we might find on these copies."

Linda hesitated. She was thinking about lawyers now. Ultimately she relented. "I guess that would be okay."

Agent Torres left to get an electronic fingerprint scanner. The electronic scanners were more accurate, required less work, and eliminated the mess of fingerprint inking. Officers also found that people were more receptive to having their fingerprints taken when the mess was eliminated.

After three exhausting hours, Linda had been through her tale four times in excruciating detail. The FBI arranged to take her back to her hotel. Unknown to her, a freelance photographer snapped her picture from across the street on her way out.

With Linda gone, Jennifer and Max sat down with Special Agent Torres. "Ok. Tell me what this is all about," the agent insisted.

Max had his head deep in the codices again so Jennifer spoke up. "We've found a book, technically a Mayan codex, just like these, at every crash site. Two were physical and one was electronic. The content of all of the others were identical to these two. The physical ones have been identical in material composition as well. Dr. Gutierrez is a specialist on all things Mayan. We're still waiting on carbon dating and other test results, but these codices are the only common denominator among the crashes."

The FBI agent looked skeptical. "I thought the whole Mayan thing stopped when the world didn't end. Plus, if passengers can buy this codex thing in airports, it's reasonable that you might find it on downed airplanes."

"Yeah, we're a long way from Mayan gods crashing airplanes, but this codex wasn't sold in the other airports. This is the only consistency we have and we can't deny that it's one hell of a coincidence. No fingerprints have been retrieved from the other codices, despite their good condition after being in a plane crash. We would really appreciate it if you would test these two codices for fingerprints. We would also like to visit the airport to see the display. Oh, we'll need to see the airport surveillance tapes from the book store where Linda picked up the codices."

"We've been told to give you any help you need so I'll get the team right on it."

Agent Torres drove Max and Jen to Austin-Bergstrom International Airport. Between the agent's FBI identification and Jen's NTSB credentials they were able to get Max through security without a ticket. It was getting late and the airport wasn't very busy with only a few flights left to go out that night. The bookstore was closed. The gate was down, but someone was still inside straightening books. The

FBI agent shook the gate and held up his credentials. "FBI," he said.

A lone, female employee approached the gate with a surly, "We're closed." It takes more than that to make the FBI go away.

"FBI and NTSB. Open the gate. If this gate isn't opened right now I promise that you'll get a full body cavity search every time you go through airport security for the rest of your life."

Grudgingly, the employee hit the button to roll up the gate. Once they were inside, she rolled it down. "How can I help the FBI today?" she asked with mock sweetness.

Jen ignored her tone. "Earlier today a woman got two free books from a display in your store. We think they may be related to yesterday's aircraft incident. Can you show us the books that look like this?" She produced one of Linda's codices.

"Um, we don't sell anything like that, and we certainly don't have any free books. This store is run by a soulless conglomerate. Nothing happens here for free." the clerk replied.

"A passenger said you had a pyramid display with free copies of this book." Jen looked around. "Right in that corner." She pointed. The spot where the codex was supposed to be contained a display with the latest Lee Child thriller in hardback.

"We need to search the store," said agent Torres.

"I'm not so sure about that," the clerk replied. "Don't you need like a warrant or something?"

"We're behind the security perimeter dear. Everything and everyone is subject to search; no warrant necessary. Now, show me your back room." He gestured to Max and Jen, "you two start out here."

Jen knew that Torres wasn't playing. There was tremendous pressure building from Washington to get this solved. They searched the little shop from top to bottom and didn't find any trace of the Mayan codex.

Jen and Max rode back to San Antonio with Special Agent Torres. Linda Welsh's story didn't check out. The best lies are built on a foundation of truth, Jen thought. Torres was going to bring Linda back in for questioning. Jennifer wasn't convinced that Linda knew anything, but she wasn't going to get in the way of the FBI.

The duo crashed for the night at the Hilton in downtown San Antonio. The FBI was sending someone to get the airport surveillance tapes, and they would go through them tomorrow.

* * *

Jen and Max were up early the next morning, eager to figure out where the books had come from.

In a conference room in the San Antonio field office, Jen found a projector set up and connected to a laptop. A very young looking agent sat behind the laptop as Special Agent Torres escorted them in.

Max was too excited to wait. "Did the surveillance tapes show the codices in the airport?" he asked.

"Yes and no. We were able to corroborate most of Ms. Welsh's story, even if you didn't find the codices yesterday. We also confirmed that the only fingerprints on both codices belonged to Ms. Welsh. Still, it's easier if you just watch the video. Tyler?" He gestured to the agent behind the laptop. The young agent cleared his throat.

"First, the shops in the airport use a closed circuit surveillance system designed to catch shoplifters, not terrorists. As part of a post 9/11 upgrade, the concourses and terminals use real time constant feeds recorded digitally to hard drives. They are archived to help identify terrorists after the fact in the event of an incident. The shops aren't as sophisticated. They use a rolling system available to the store clerks as well as the airport police. In the bookstore, three cameras cycle through the store spending fifteen seconds on each location. There is some overlap so the longest any location is completely off camera is fifteen seconds. Everyone clear?"

The room nodded as the agent queued up the footage. The video was fuzzy so the young agent narrated along with the images.

"Here we have the store. There is the corner with the Lee Child book pyramid. The camera angle isn't great, but you can just see the edge of the cover. No codex." The footage flashed to a different angle. "Here is the front of the store, now it's off camera for fifteen seconds. Finally, here comes our subject."

The group watched Linda walk into the frame.

"Our subject goes over to the Lee Child pyramid. kShe flips through a book and walks halfway toward the register. She asks the clerk something."

He paused the video.

"Based on the subject's statement, this is where she would have asked if the codex was free. Notice, the subject did not get close enough to exchange anything with the salesperson. The salesperson was distracted. She never looks up. Our suspect did not pay for the book. No cash, no card, nothing. Now it gets weird." He pressed play. "The subject walks back and, in full view of the salesperson, puts two books in her bag. He paused again. The screen froze on a shot of one book, just as it started to enter the bag."

Max stared at the image. "The book is wrong," he said.

"Bingo," replied the agent.

"Leave it to the book guy to spot that," muttered Jennifer quietly, half kidding. The FBI agent switched the display to show an enlarged version of the shot.

"The tech guys finished enlarging and enhancing this image about a half hour ago," the agent said.

The enlarged imaged showed the cover of the Mayan codex they were all coming to know so well. Linda was placing it in her bag.

# 8.

"WAIT, WHEN DID THE BOOK change?" asked Jennifer.

"We're handicapped by the quality of the video, but it's one book on the table and another book in the bag," offered the agent. With that he rewound and replayed the video multiple times. "We went through this a dozen times this morning already and either this lady is a magician pulling a slight of hand trick or someone tampered with the recording."

The little group watched the video another twenty times. It was eighteen times through before Max noticed the clock. "Wait," he said. "Slow it down and watch the clock in the corner."

They watched a wall clock on the video. The hands moved in time with the video images. Max continued. "The wall clock stays in tune with the video. There's no missing time. That's the kind of detail that is way too easy to miss. I'm not sure that this video has been tampered with."

The young FBI agent was indignant. "What other explanation is there? I assume you're not suggesting that the book magically appeared? It's more likely that Ms. Welsh walked in with it in her bag and made up this whole story for publicity. "

"I don't know what I'm suggesting, but it's getting harder to believe that the video was tampered with this professionally in such a short amount of time." Max's retort was weak and he knew it, but tampering with the video so perfectly just didn't seem possible. After all, the FBI had the video less than twenty four hours after the crash.

Jen jumped in. "None of this makes sense. We haven't mentioned the book as a link to the press. If Linda is just hunting for publicity, how did she know about the book? If she planted the codex, where did she get it from? Why crash a plane that you are on? For that matter how did she crash it?" Jen was almost shouting now.

Agent Torres responded, "We're bringing Linda back in for another interview. Frankly, it doesn't make sense to us either, yet. There's nothing in her background to suggest that she has anything to do with this, so we're going lean on her and see what happens."

At noon a disheartened Max and Jennifer headed back to their hotel for lunch.

People love a good conspiracy theory, and with nothing better coming from the government, an enterprising reporter had put the photos of Linda leaving the FBI together with her video proclaiming the codex as the source of the crashes. That tenuous connection was all it took for the story to go viral.

The bar at the Hilton doubled as a restaurant. Max held out a bar stool for Jen and they ordered a pair of burgers. Fox News was on the TV and the screen showed a plane crash graphic next to the talking head. Jennifer had the bartender turn it up.

"...from San Antonio we've learned that the FBI questioned passenger Linda Welsh for several hours. Sources indicate that the questioning centered on her claim that a book led to the emergency landing of Unified Air flight 3675. A YouTube video showing her holding the book after the flight has gone viral." The graphic hovering next to the anchor woman's head morphed into a grainy copy of the codex's cover.

Jennifer's phone rang. It was Ed Rollins.

"Turn on Fox News," was his greeting.

"Already watching," she said.

"We are having an all hands meeting with the various crash teams in D.C. tomorrow. Be there and bring the codex guy. Details are in your email."

Jen hung up and turned to Max. "We are going to Washington. You've been promoted to a full member of the team."

They checked out and headed for the airport with Jennifer driving. Max finished passing on their plans to Agent Torres when his phone rang. "Yes. Uh huh. You're sure? Both of them? What's the range?"

Jen was only getting part of the conversation, but Max was becoming more agitated as the call went on. Finally he hung up.

"That was the lab that is carbon dating the codices. They say that both of the codices date to somewhere between 10 BC and 10 AD and yes, they are sure."

\* \* \*

"CNN has confirmed that officials at both the FBI and the NTSB believe that there is some link between this mysterious book, what officials are calling a 'codex', and the recent rash of airliner crashes. They are quick to clarify that they don't believe that the book is the cause of the crash, but it may be a signature of some type," said this half hour's talking head. "Up next, are aircraft manufacturers too involved in accident investigations? And do their political donations help cover up problems? We'll tackle those questions and more up next on..."

In the Oval Office, the President waved at the TV. His Chief of Staff muted the set, silencing the CNN anchor in mid-sentence.

This was an intimate meeting with just his Chief of Staff and National Security Advisor. "Why did we just inform the public that we have a serial killer in the air?" asked the President.

The question hung between them as both advisers struggled for an answer.

The Chief of Staff found his voice first. "Mr. President I don't believe that's what we did..."

The President cut him off. "When you use the word 'signature' the American people think serial killer. We've drilled that into their heads over and over again with TV and movies. It doesn't matter what the real meaning is, that's what it means to the public. We're gearing up for an election and these plane crashes have both national security and economic implications. It took years for the airlines to recover from 9/11. Now that they are finally running at capacity, every crash kills hundreds. I am not going to be the President that doesn't get reelected because he can't stop airplanes from falling out of the sky!"

By the time he finished the President found himself shouting. Clearly he was worried. The President took a deep breath to calm down. He asked, "Where are we on this? Do we have any idea what's bringing down these planes?"

The National Security Advisor cleared his throat. "The FBI and NTSB are meeting on this now. Everyone agrees that there haven't been any explosives. The planes are simply coming apart. The problem is that there is no consistency. Since Boeing and Airbus are the two major manufacturers there is always a risk that a crash could involve one of their planes. But we've seen problems with Boeing, Airbus, and Embraer. Embraer is a Brazilian manufacturer of small, regional jets. The range of companies leads us to believe it is not a manufacturing problem. Also we've seen everything from wide body aircraft to fifty seat regional jets.

The NTSB is looking at maintenance records. Originally, they suspected a maintenance problem with Fiesta Air. But the Triangle crash is a different story. Triangle Air got busted and fined heavily for maintenance problems two years ago. The fine wiped out their quarterly profit and led to the CEO's

resignation. Ever since then they've have had a spot-
less maintenance record. Also, we're talking about
multiple airlines as well. We shouldn't see catastrophic maintenance failures from multiple airlines."

"So the FBI has the investigation now?" asked the
President.

"Yes sir," replied the Chief of Staff. "Once the
team found a common element, even a bizarre element like this codex, it made sense to hand over the
investigation to the FBI. The NTSB is still assisting."

"What about the allegations that the manufacturers are too close?"

Again the Chief of Staff replied "Mr. President,
these are incredibly complex machines. This isn't
like a car crash. Without the help of the manufacturers many of these crashes would never be solved.
The manufacturer's involvement is a red herring, as
is the political angle. What about our other pro-
posal?"

The President stood up and paced while his
Chief of Staff and National Security Advisor sat on
the couch. In the Oval Office only the President
paced.

"Mr. President, this is the only way. We have to
ban this book or codex or whatever it is from airplanes. We'll tighten TSA procedures and have them

look for it. It will play havoc with security lines, but that's better than shutting down air travel." The Chief of Staff hoped he would go for it. The President was getting crucified in the polls. He had to do something.

"I don't like the idea of banning a book. It goes against everything we stand for in this country. The ACLU will crucify me. The religious right will claim banning the Bible is next."

The Chief of Staff waved this away. "Mr. President, you aren't banning a book. You're looking for evidence of a terrorist signature. We prevent all kinds of things on airplanes now. We're just adding one more thing. This is more like steps we've taken to limit gang symbols in schools than banning a book."

The President sighed in resignation. The Chief of Staff knew he had won.

"Ok, have TSA look for the book. I still think it's stupid. Most TSA agents can't find their own ass on a good day, but at least it looks like we're doing something." The President stopped and turned to his Chief of Staff. "This is going to cost you. If I'm banning this codex thing I want Lizard on the investigation."

His Chief of Staff went white, but before he could stammer out an objection the President interrupted.

"No buts. I want Lizard on this, not in the lead of course, I can't survive that kind of press, but make sure the FBI knows she's coming. Give her whatever she needs."

\* \* \*

The NTSB team leads from the various crashes met in a large, auditorium style room at the NTSB headquarters on L'Enfant Plaza in Washington, D.C. Ed Rollins chaired the meeting. On the stage, Ed spoke into the microphone, trying to quiet everyone down.

"All right everyone, simmer down, simmer down." The room grew quiet. "You are all aware by now that the FBI has taken the lead on these crashes. They've concluded that the codex that has been found at the scene of all four crashes represents a signature. That's not conclusive evidence of a crime, but the President has determined that it's enough to hand the investigation over to the FBI. However, we're not done. We still owe it to the American public to find out the cause of these crashes. We are going to figure out what is bringing down these planes. Once that happens, the FBI can figure out who is responsible."

He turned to a man in a suit standing behind him to his right. "Speaking of the FBI, let me introduce

Supervisory Special Agent Sidney Graham. He will be overseeing the investigation."

SSA Graham stepped up to the microphone. As Jennifer sat with Max on right side of the room, she decided that she didn't like Agent Graham. He looks like a weasel, she thought. Intellectually, she knew that this was just a reaction to the FBI taking over their case. Still, his slick hair and expensive suit should go over well with the engineers in the room, she thought sarcastically.

Jennifer's thoughts went back to what SSA Graham was saying. "...at the FBI, we too are committed to finding out who is behind these attacks. I've been assured that we have the full weight of the United States government behind this investigation. We will get to the bottom of it and we will need your help."

It was a rah-rah speech. Jen suspected that privately, Agent Graham would be happy to solve this one and take the credit with or without the NTSB. "Win one for the Gipper," she whispered to Max. He chuckled.

Ed took the floor from the agent and looked out at the room. "For the next four hours we're going to split up. Each of the major sections will meet in separate conference rooms to look for commonalities. I want all of the structural engineers comparing notes.

Same thing for power plant, flight ops, you name it. I know that some of you are very early in your investigations, but we want to cross reference everything. Maybe it will give you something to look for when you get back. After lunch we'll meet back here to review as a group."

The room split up. Jen headed for the Flight Operations room. Max walked away.

"Hey, where are you going?" she called.

"I have calls to make. I can't contribute to any of these discussions. Maybe I can be useful on the phone."

They had talked a little about the codex and its age on the flight to D.C. A female passenger kept shooting them dirty looks from across the aisle as they talked about the codex and its link to the crashes. They decided to quit before she complained to a flight attendant.

* * *

Four hours later, at lunch, Jennifer complained to Max that her session hadn't made any progress. "There is nothing flight control related in these crashes. Ed's grasping at straws."

"I don't have anything either," replied Max. "I spent the last four hours running down the battery on my cell phone talking to other Mayan experts.

The bill from the Dresden call is going to be a bitch when it comes in next month. I expect to submit it to the NTSB for reimbursement. Anyway, all of it was for nothing. Nobody has any real idea how a pristine codex ends up in a plane crash, not to mention multiple codices and multiple crashes."

They were mostly done eating and still had half an hour before the afternoon session. Jen leaned back in her chair and took a bite of banana pudding. She looked at Max, "Speculate. What are any of the ways that a codex could end up in a crash? Don't worry about how crazy they are for now."

Gutierrez put his elbows on the table. "For just one codex, it could have been in a private collection for years, kept in perfect humidity to prevent decay, and never revealed. The owner was on the plane that crashed and we got lucky. That doesn't work for multiple codices though."

Jen frowned. "Hey no judgments."

Max teased. "You said no matter how crazy."

He ticked off a few more. "One, same scenario, but the person with the codex is a master thief. Two, maybe a master forger has decided to flood the market with fakes as payback for something. Three, maybe someone on that flight stole Q'uq'umatz's sacred book and he wants it back. I don't know." He threw up his hands in frustration. "I don't know how you get four, identical Mayan codices when only three unique ones have ever been found in the world up until now. Throw in the electronic one and I'm really lost. The Maya were advanced but not that advanced. Maybe someone is running around planting perfectly fake codices on plane crash sites before you get there."

Max looked at Jen. "Your turn. How do you rip wings off a plane at altitude in stable flight without explosives?"

Jen thought about it. "I've got nothing. Even with sabotage, at level flight it's unlikely that cracks in the wings would cause them to come off. That's more likely with the stresses caused during takeoff and landing. You didn't even mention the can opener scenario. Cylinders don't peel open. The physics don't work that way. I'm stumped."

The rest of the day was just as unproductive.

# 9.

L AKISHA JONES WAS A NERVOUS FLYER, but her mother was having cancer treatments and needed her help, so Lakisha was going home. She boarded an ancient Discount Air DC-9 in Newark bound for Jackson, Mississippi. At eighteen, she had left Mississippi for college on the east coast. She wanted more opportunities than Mississippi had to offer a young black woman. Ten years later she was still looking for those opportunities. The cost of living near New York was outrageous and seemed to chew up every dime she made. That led her to pick Discount Air. It was the cheapest option to get back to what she still thought of as home.

As Lakisha took her seat, she cinched her seat belt until it was almost too tight. She had paid extra for an exit row seat on the aisle. As she settled her top heavy frame between the armrests she thought about the extra fifty dollars she had paid for the seat. Lakisha resented that she had to pay for a seat assignment, but she didn't regret it. With the extra room in the exit row, maybe now the tray table won't hit me in the chest, she thought.

Lakisha paid careful attention to the flight attendant's instructions. Obviously the nearest exit was the window to her left, followed by the window to her right. Same thing one row up. The front of the plane was seventeen rows forward and the rear exit was nine rows back. "Not good enough," she muttered to herself.

"What was that?" her seat mate asked. He looked like he was in his late forties with a flannel shirt, jeans, and a Bass Pro Shop cap. Mississippi Redneck going home, Lakisha thought. She didn't mind rednecks, she'd grown up with plenty of them in Mississippi. Like every other class of people, some were extremely nice, others were assholes. New York didn't have a lot of rednecks, but there was no shortage of assholes. This guy seemed okay so far.

"Nothing really," she replied. "I just read this article that said that your best chance of getting out of a plane crash is to be within 8 rows of an exit. If we can't get out these window exits for some reason we probably aren't getting out."

"Now don't worry about that. I'm not dying on no airplane." With that he pulled down his cap and went to sleep.

Lakisha paid close attention to the flight attendant's announcement. She found herself fixated on the life vests. "Under the seat, over the head, around the waist, pull the tabs..." She repeated this like a mantra, even though the flight would take place entirely over land. "Under the seat, over the head, around the waist, pull the tabs..."

Discount Air was about as discount as air travel can get. They were regularly fined by the FAA for safety issues. When the oldest planes in their fleet hit a significant maintenance milestone they would dump the aircraft and buy another clunker. It was cheaper to buy and refit something discarded by another airline than to take their aircraft through the required recertification tests, so that's what they did.

Even with Discount Air's maintenance issues and the heightened concerns about flying, it was a surprise when twenty minutes into the flight everyone heard a loud bang and the plane rolled to the left. Books and music players flew and showered Lakisha and the rest of the left side passengers. A heavy roller board suitcase launched out of the overhead bin above the right side of row twelve and knocked the lady sitting in seat 12C unconscious. Drink service had just started so the heavy drink cart was out. It crushed the leg of the man in 3C. If the plane inverted it would likely kill everyone in the row.

All three flight attendants were down. One had bounced her head against an overhead bin and was unconscious. Another was sprawled across the laps of the passengers in aisle six. The third one was crumpled against a door in the galley. Amid the screams of the passengers, the pilot and copilot wrestled for control of the airplane.

Their effort was rewarded when the plane finally stopped its roll. The ancient DC-9 was precariously perched at a forty-five degree angle with passengers clawing at seat backs, desperately trying to avoid sliding out of their seat belts. In the cockpit, pilot Scott Carlson was barking orders through gritted teeth as he fought the control yoke. "I've got the airplane," he said to the copilot. "See if you can figure out what's wrong."

Airplanes have checklists for everything. With the captain locked in a death match with the controls, the copilot checked the instruments, warning lights, and settings. "Alright, first guess is an uncommanded slats deployment," was the reply. "I can try resetting the slats, but if it works you're going to be overcompensating."

"Try it," came the grunted reply. The copilot deployed and reset the slats. As the slats retracted the plane snapped sharply back to the right. The pilot let go of the control yoke to allow the autopilot to automatically right the plane, but it didn't come all the way back. There was still a slight list to the left. The captain trimmed the plane to compensate and bring them back into level flight. "It feels like the slats didn't completely retract, but we've got the airplane back. Let's update the Mayday and get this thing on the ground," the captain said. "Start the emergency landing checklist."

Lakisha was in full panic mode now. The plane had snapped left and stayed there. She had nearly crushed her seatmate. Just when she was getting worried about his breathing, the plane swung back to the right. The move was violent enough that some passengers slammed their heads against the windows. A minute or two later the screams subsided as they came back to more or less level flight. Lakisha was glad for the reinforced armrests in the exit rows. She was sure that she would have ripped off a regular armrest in panic. Finally, she heard an announcement from the captain.

"Ladies and gentlemen," the captain began. "We believe that we just suffered a mechanical issue that caused the plane to lurch like it did. We have declared an emergency and are diverting to Philadelphia, the nearest major airfield. Please remain in your seats with your seatbelt securely fastened and follow all crew instructions. We don't know what damage we've sustained so we expect to use the emergency exits to evacuate the aircraft. Please review the safety brochures in the seat pockets in front of you and follow all flight attendant instructions. As we approach for landing, we will want everyone in brace position."

A few minutes later, they had a still unconscious flight attendant strapped into a seat. One flight attendant had a broken arm, but thought that she could still open the forward door. She was strapped in up front. The other flight attendant walked to the back to be ready to release the tail cone and rear slide.

On her way to the back, the flight attendant stopped at the emergency exit rows for a quick briefing. "We're down a flight attendant, so you'll have to open the window exits," she began. "Get in the brace position for landing. After we stop, pull the release to expose the actual emergency handle. Pull down on the handle and push in to free the exit door. Use the grip on the bottom with your other hand and throw the door out the window. There is no slide on the wing. With the flaps down you won't be that far from the ground. The engines are up on the tail in this aircraft so they won't pose a danger to you. Slide down the wing in a sitting position and move away from the aircraft. Don't wait at the bottom or people will crash into you." She confirmed that the rows on each side had heard her and moved to take her position in the back.

Lakisha listened intently, but all that went through her head was "Under the seat, over the head, around the waist, pull the tabs..."

The wounded Discount Air DC-9 rattled in for a landing. Passengers were bent over with their head between their knees in the crash position. As the pilot floated the landing, fire trucks roared along parallel to, and slightly behind, the wobbly bird. Captain Carlson brought her down with a thump, a nasty wobble, and then a nice long run. When they finally stopped some passengers jumped out of their seats. Others sat in a daze, unwilling or unable to move. The flight attendants called for evacuation. Lakisha's seat mate grabbed the handles and started working on the door.

Lakisha panicked. As she jumped up, she reached under her seat and grabbed her life vest. She placed it over her head. Over the head, around the waist, pull..., she thought. As soon as the door went out the window, Lakisha pull the tab on her life vest to inflate it. The redneck went out the window exit and gallantly stopped on the wing to help others out. Lakisha moved toward the open window. Between her bulk and the life vest, she promptly got stuck in the exit window.

Passengers piled up behind her pushing and shoving. She kept trying to wriggle her way through, but she was stuck like a cork in champagne bottle. Finally, she twisted just enough, and the crowd pushed just hard enough, that Lakisha popped through the door, rolled on to the wing and tumbled to the ground.

She landed face down, the life vest, and her ample chest, kept her face from slamming into the tarmac. The life vest burst and air hissed out as she hit. With the life vest slowly deflating, she stopped with her face inches from the ground. Realizing she was alive, Lakisha bent down and kissed the concrete. She was alive, even if she was in Philadelphia.

* * *

"Yes, yes, no sign of a codex. Got it. Thanks Ed." Jen hung up the phone. She and Max were back in Nashville trying to brainstorm anything that could help solve these crashes. The NTSB hated it when things got handed over to the FBI. Jen turned to Max. "That was Ed Rollins. Discount Air appears to have just been poor maintenance. No sign of a codex. That may be the end of Discount Air, but at least all the passengers survived. It sucks for the pilot though. He did everything right, and he's still probably going to be out of a job."

"That and it does nothing for us," Max replied. The Discount Air story was on the TV Max kept in the corner of his office. They had muted it when Jen's cell phone rang.

"There is just no way to reconcile the facts," Max argued. They had been rehashing the evidence. "One codex, in perfect shape, the right age, everything, maybe, maybe, I could believe that. But not multiple exact duplicates."

Jen responded, "But that's what we have, and as Sherlock Holmes said..."

"Yes, yes, 'when you have excluded the impossible, whatever remains, however improbable, must be the truth.'" He said, finishing the Doyle quote. "I've heard it before. The problem is that all we have on these crashes is the impossible."

A graphic of a codex appeared on the TV. Jennifer turned it up. "...The President banned the carrying of a Mayan codex on aircraft today. The ACLU immediately condemned the practice and promised to sue on first amendment grounds. Religious leaders also expressed concern about banning what some view as a sacred text."

The scene cut away to show protesters as the voice over said, "Latino groups protested the decision to ban the codex, calling the Mayan books 'a crucial element of Hispanic heritage'. The President's press secretary tried to diffuse the furor at today's press conference."

The broadcast cut away to show a man in a suit reading a prepared statement to the press. "We are not banning Mayan codices. We are simply preventing passengers from carrying them on to aircraft, much as we do with weapons, flammable objects, and knives."

A headline banner ran below the press conference with other breaking news. A long dormant volcano was showing signs of life in the Mexican state of Campeche, southwest of Cancun.

* * *

A local, short-term storage facility in East St. Louis, Illinois was an odd place to setup a terrorist organization, but the place was quiet, secure, and they took cash. That's why Omar used it as the base for his terrorist organization, the Fist of Allah.

Omar didn't look much like a terrorist either. He was taller than average, a little over six feet, with only a mustache on his face. The pullover golf shirt and khakis he wore certainly didn't portray a sinister image. Omar's little band was similarly groomed and dressed. Only Mohammed sported a well-trimmed beard.

Omar was the general manager of a small shipping company. Mohammed worked as a mechanical engineer. Kaseem managed a large consumer warehouse store, and Habib was legally a student, though he had stopped attending classes some time ago.

They had met at a local mosque. Despite their differences in age and background, they all harbored a deep resentment toward the United States. Out of that resentment had come the Fist of Allah.

Omar had rented the largest storage unit the company offered. The front of the unit was stuffed with cast off furniture to make the unit appear full. Behind the first layer of junk, however, the unit contained weapons, a small fold out table, and four chairs. Omar had intentionally kept this cell small. Just himself and his three associates.

Kaseem travelled to Canada occasionally as part of his job. He made contact with a radical group in

Toronto with ties to Pakistan. They got the weapons into Canada. Omar used the trucking firm he worked for to get them across the border and into the United States.

So far, Omar's little band hadn't done any damage to the great Satan, the United States. They spent a lot of time talking and very little time doing. Tonight's meeting was designed to change that. Assault rifles and rocket launchers weren't enough to strike a crushing blow. They now had a weapon at their disposal to deliver a fatal blow to the Americans.

Omar looked at his little group. Like Omar, Mohammad and Kaseem had families and, despite their devotion to Allah, Omar worried about their commitment to a suicide mission. He decided that this job would fall to Habib. Now it was time to rile them up.

Standing before them, Omar began, "My brothers." He paused for effect. "We now have an opportunity to strike at the great Satan. This mystery book that we have seen on the news is causing planes to crash in the United States. Though it is a blasphemous book of an infidel god, it appears to have power over the great Satan's aircraft."

The rollup door was closed to prevent eavesdropping and it was starting to get uncomfortably warm in the storage unit. Omar bent over and removed something from the bag he had brought with him. With a bead of sweat on his forehead, he lifted a Mayan codex over his head. "Allah has given us a weapon with which to strike at America!"

The small group gasped. Omar might as well have been holding an atomic bomb. He'd actually stolen the codex from a display at Barnes & Noble. When he'd turned back for another, the books were gone. Given the mood that the FBI was in, simply having this book could get Omar arrested and locked up for questioning.

"I have heard from Allah that we are to strike against the great Satan, and the tip of our sword is to be Habib."

Habib was sweating now, and it had nothing to do with a closed rollup door. He wasn't sure he wanted to be the tip of the sword. Still, Habib would do what was required of him.

\* \* \*

Jen and Max walked back to Max's bookstore after a late dinner. They'd been spending an awful lot of time together trying to solve the mystery of these crashes. Jen was finding that she didn't mind spending time with Max. He wasn't an aviation buff, but he was smart and funny, in a self-effacing way. The bookstore was dark as Max unlocked the door. Jen flipped on the lights to find someone already inside. Sitting in arm chair in the corner was a dark figure, clad in black leather, with its head down.

The figure raised it head and spoke. "It's about time you guys got back. Are we trying to prevent plane crashes, or is this some kind of NTSB dating game?"

Max took a step back. "And just who the hell do you think you are breaking into my bookstore?"

The figure stood up. In the gloom Max got a glimpse of dark hair and dark eyes. As it stepped forward, Max was surprised to see that it was a woman, and a very young looking one at that. "I'm special agent Lizard Wong, Homeland Security." She didn't hold out her hand. Max stuck his out, more out of reflex than anything else. The agent ignored it.

Special Agent Wong didn't look like someone from Homeland Security. Her bangs swept down over one eye. The leather jacket, black jeans, and skull t-shirt made Max think of a biker chick. The lip stud, nose ring, and dark eye makeup added a vaguely gothic look. Slightly almond eyes hinted at Asian ancestry, but he couldn't be sure. Absentmindedly, he wondered if she had a dragon tattoo. "Since when is Homeland Security hiring twelve year old Marilyn Manson wannabes?"

Lizard looked hard at Max, then smiled. "I like you. You've got spunk for a bookstore owner. You are allowed to call me Lizard. Besides, Marilyn Manson wishes he looked this good."

Lizard showed her badge to Max and Jen and then pointedly handed her card to Jen, snubbing Max. Max looked doubtful. "The FBI already has the case," he said. "Why do we need Homeland Security too?"

"I'm not here to work with the FBI. I get called in to chase the more...shall we say unusual...occurrences," she replied.

"Unusual? Like magically appearing books that shouldn't exist?" asked Jen. "Or like vampires and werewolves unusual?"

"All of the above, but I don't do pretty, teeny-bopper vampires. Twilight made me want to throw up. Most of the things I investigate turn out to be nothing but fakes, hoaxes or delusions."

A wry smile spread on Max's face. "So you're the ..."

"Yes, I'm the Scooby Doo of Homeland Security." Lizard scowled. She did not look happy.

"I was going to say X-Files, but Scooby Doo will work." Max was grinning like a cat now.

Lizard tightened her scowl. "Ok, now you can call me Agent Wong. When Homeland security was formed the FBI couldn't wait to get rid of our little group." She pulled out a forty-five caliber Glock 21SF and gestured with it toward Max. "However, I'm armed and kind of sensitive about the whole thing."

He held up his hands in mock surrender. The few FBI agents he'd met so far had been arrogant robots. This crazy Homeland Security agent was at least interesting.

Jen interrupted. "Wait. You said, 'most of the time'. What does that mean?"

Lizard put her gun away. "It means that in spite all of the con men, wannabe YouTube stars, and plain old nut jobs, we can't always explain everything. Call the numbers on my card or lookup Homeland Security phone numbers on the internet. Check on my status. Everyone always does. I'll be disappointed if you don't. I live for the look on people's faces when they find out the badge is real."

Max took the card from Jen, picked up the phone, and dialed. While he was on hold, Max studied this "Lizard" person that had invaded his store. She really does look like a twelve year old mall rat, he thought. Ok, twelve is unfair, maybe nineteen on a good day. Didn't you have to be older than that to be a Homeland Security Agent?

Half an hour later, Max and Jen were satisfied that the dark apparition that had invaded the bookstore really was a Homeland Security agent. Agent Wong used the time to field strip and clean her Glock while watching CNN. Jen and Max sat down across from her. "It's starting," Wong said, her eyes on the TV.

"What's starting?" asked Jen.

"The panic."

# 10.

SiX HOURS EARLIER, TWENTY YEAR OLD Cameron Washburn was on a bus to Fargo, North Dakota. He'd left Nebraska to try to find work in the shale oil fields. North Dakota was booming with high paying jobs for those with the right skills. He figured that he could work a year or two to get the skills he needed and then move up. College was never his thing. He preferred to be outdoors. The pay in North Dakota wasn't quite up there with Alaska pipeline or gulf oil rig work, but it wasn't quite as dangerous either.

Uncharacteristically, the Greyhound was full. Of course he got stuck next to the old guy who wouldn't shut up.

"... yesiree, I'm not flying anymore," he half heard the old man say. "TSA was trampling my rights before, but now it's just ridiculous. Folks have to put all their books in the stupid plastic bins with their toiletries. Plus they have to let TSA search their electronics for digital copies of this codex thing. TSA's not getting their hands on my iPad that's for sure."

Cameron raised his head, uncrossed his arms, and sat up. This old fart can't spell iPad, not to mention how to use one, he thought. If the old geezer wasn't going shut up and he wasn't going to get any sleep, he might as well read something. Cameron reached beneath the seat in front of him and pulled out a comic book. He was still working his way through the full Walking Dead series. It took a full five minutes for the old man to notice.

"Hey, what you got there kid? That's not a codex is it?"

What? Thought Cameron. What kind of moron would confuse a comic book with a codex? He turned to respond to the old man, but he wasn't prepared for the reaction of the other passengers.

"A codex? He's trying to crash the bus!" yelled an overweight man in a cowboy hat.

A trailer park blonde turned to look at him from three rows ahead. She screamed, "Terrorist fucker!" and tossed an unopened Diet Coke can at him. It struck him in the cheek. Cameron wasn't sure if he was more stunned by the full soda can or by the vitriol over a mistaken book.

Now everyone was yelling and screaming except the teenage couple in the back. They'd lit a joint earlier and were still out.

This isn't happening thought Cameron. Behind him he heard "let's roll" and a huge black man pulled him out of his aisle seat and on to the floor. Cameron curled into a ball trying to protect his head as the larger passenger started beating him. The rest of the bus tried to squeeze into the small space to pile on. As the bus driver finally moved to pull over, a teenager in the front seat, stepped into the space next to the driver and dove into the pile. In the process he kicked the bus driver in the head causing the bus to swerve off the road and into a ditch.

* * *

As the CNN story on Cameron's ordeal finished, Wong muted the sound. "What they didn't say is that he had a Walking Dead comic book, nothing like a codex. Plus the wings can come off a bus all day long and it won't crash. This wasn't a terrorist attack or supernatural event. This was a group panic attack, and if the bus hadn't crashed, that poor shmuck would be dead. We're going to see more of this if we don't stop whoever or whatever is doing this, so I'd like to understand what you know."

Jen and Max spent an hour on the basics. Since it was late, they agreed to meet the next morning to dig into the details.

* * *

It proved to be ridiculously easy to get the codex past airport security. Habib used a book cover left over from his time in college to cover the codex. He hand labeled it "Financial Accounting II" and doodled on the cover in a way that he hoped would seem like the bored ramblings of a college student. Apparently financial accounting was not TSA's strong suit because they didn't give the codex a second glance. Now he was in an aisle seat on AmerAir flight 1067 from Chicago to Los Angeles. He had driven to Chicago from East St. Louis, counting on O'Hare's chaotic security to work in Allah's favor.

Flight 1067 was a six AM flight designed to use the time zone differences to get business people to Los Angeles in time for a full day of work. Despite the recent disasters, the flight was packed. There was still business to be done on the west coast. Omar had discussed with Habib the best time to bring down the flight, but none of them quite knew what Habib needed to do to use the book to crash the plane. Allah would have to provide.

Habib waited until they were about an hour into to the flight. He'd been sweating nervously and fidgeting. The members of the Fist of Allah had read all they could about Air Marshals and Omar believed that the chances of encountering one on any given flight was slim. Besides, once the book was already on board the plane, what could an Air Marshall do? Shoot it? Omar had been right. There was no Air Marshal aboard flight 1067. Habib couldn't know that and still didn't know what to do. He took a deep breath and chose the bold route.

Habib removed the codex from his carryon bag. He slipped off the book cover and stood up in the aisle. He raised the codex over his head shouted. "I am the Fist of Allah," he began. "Death to America! With this book I will crash this plane."

The reaction of the passengers was immediate, stunned silence followed by screaming and a rush of passengers trying to tackle, and then dismember, Habib.

Robert Weldon was a former Marine and now a Chicago cop. He was headed to L.A. for a conference. Robert had noticed the sweaty, fidgety Habib and his combined marine and cop senses were on high alert. Consequently, Robert got to Habib first. Habib didn't realize that a person's face could be pushed that far into the thin airliner carpet, but the ex-Marine was trying to push Habib's face through the floor of the plane. Nor did Habib realize that his arm would bend that way. The searing pain told him it wasn't supposed to.

Habib was actually subdued quickly. It took a lot longer to get all of the passengers who wanted a shot at him back in their seats. The captain declared an emergency and headed for the nearest airport of any size. Lincoln, Nebraska was about to become a media circus.

Omar anticipated that there could be problems. Habib could get caught with the book at security. He could get cold feet. The plane could survive. It was time to move. As soon as Habib left, the remaining Fist of Allah members started emptying the storage unit into a truck Omar had borrowed from work.

* * *

Jen, Max, and Lizard met that morning at Max's bookstore. Max confirmed Lizard's credentials again. He was convinced that he had dreamed the whole thing the night before. Lizard brought doughnuts. With a doughnut in hand, Jen realized how many runs she had missed since this mess had started. CNN was still on. The attempted terrorist attack and the capture of Habib was all over the news.

"So that's it. It was terrorists," said Max.

"Nope," Lizard responded succinctly.

Jen agreed, but she wasn't just going to let Lizard win without a good reason. "What makes you say that?"

Lizard held a doughnut between the thumb and forefinger of her left hand. With her right hand she started counting off the reasons.

"First, how did they bring down the other planes? No explosives were found remember? Second, how did they get the books in bookstores? I saw the same Austin airport security video that you did. Finally, if they were responsible for the other crashes, why couldn't they crash this plane? If you're a terrorist and you know how to rip the wings off an airplane in mid-flight without a bomb, you do it. You don't blow it and get caught. I think this is a failed copycat.

I'll touch base with the FBI later, but for now I'd like you to walk me through everything. We're going to do this in excruciating detail. Even if it is terrorism, we may need this for the prosecution."

"Ok, I don't have anything better to do. Let's go through it again," said Jen.

"Let's start with the first flight. It's the only one with a Mexican angle. Maybe the Mayan stuff got started there."

The three of them talked through the flight and finding the first codex.

"What about the Fiesta Air 169 manifest?" Wong asked.

"We looked at everyone," Jen commented. "We had time between the crashes and we dug into everyone's background. The plane was full of tourists, plain and simple."

"What about those tourists? What did they do in Mexico? I want to tear apart this first flight. This thing started there and my gut tells me the answer is there too."

Jen worked her way down the list of passengers. With a hundred and sixty people to go through, it took all day. In the weeks following the crash they had pulled the itineraries, hotel records, Jet Ski rentals, everything, for every passenger. When they got to the Raintrees Jen stopped.

"Hmmm ... that's different. Most of the tourists just hung around the hotel. They went parasailing, jet skiing, you name it. A few took the bus into the market in town, or made day trips to nearby ruins, but most folks just stayed on property at their hotel in and around Cancun. Cancun is pretty safe, but the media reports of drug cartel violence have been keeping people in. We do have one family that left the reservation. The Raintree family stayed outside of the normal tourist areas. They rented a car and drove almost three hundred miles southwest to stay at some kind of eco-resort. They hired a local guide through the hotel to take them out to some ruins in the middle of the jungle. "

Wong arched an eyebrow and looked at Max. "That ring any ancient codex bells for you?"

Max snapped his fingers. "Calakmul!" he exclaimed. Max saw the quizzical looks on Jen and Lizard's faces. "Calakmul is an ancient Mayan ruin. It was discovered in 1930 and all but forgotten until 1982. It's not touristy, and large areas of it still aren't fully documented."

Jen checked her notes. "It says they stayed at the Hotel Puerta Calakmul. That's who arranged the guide too. Wait, didn't a volcano start acting up near there recently?" Jen had watched so much CNN from the plane crashes lately that she could repeat a half hour headline segment from memory.

"Ok, so we have a place to start," Wong said. "Look, I think we need to tackle the elephant in the room. Most of my investigations start with something paranormal, but they don't end that way. I'm not Mulder from the X Files. I'm closer to Scully.

I'm the skeptic. In this case though, I'm starting to believe that there could be a supernatural element here."

"I'm a long way from that," said Max.

Jen agreed with Max. "Look, it's been a long day, can we get some dinner and fight about supernatural elements over food?"

They ate at a little Italian place down the block.

Jen tried to be polite. She turned to Lizard and asked, "So how did you end up ... ah?" She was at a loss for words.

Lizard jumped in, "a Scooby Doo?"

They all chuckled.

"I was a relatively new FBI agent doing grunt work on a case. I'd transferred out of sex crimes and was assisting on a case involving a serial killer who thought he was a werewolf. The local FBI SSA, that's supervisory special agent, dismissed the whole thing as a hoax. He sent me in just to shut up the locals. I tracked the guy down and figured out that he wasn't a werewolf after all."

"How did you decide that he wasn't a werewolf?" asked Jen.

"I shot him repeatedly and he died. It didn't even take a silver bullet to kill him. Regular bullets worked just fine, but I bent a few rules along the way. Apparently I have a problem with authority. Who knew?" She smiled menacingly.

Max and Jen chuckled.

"Actually I have a problem with idiots in authority. If it was just a problem with authority they would have figured that out at the FBI academy and kicked me out at that point. You would think that catching serial killers is good for an FBI career, but apparently showing up your boss offsets shooting serial killers. So I got transferred to an underfunded, overlooked division that investigates the oddball cases that no one wants.

Our little freak squad is generally idiot free. Now that we're under Homeland Security instead of the FBI it's even easier to hide out. There's less oversight and a bigger budget. Homeland Security wastes money like a former Disney child star on crack. Of course, TSA is part of Homeland Security so on the whole, we've got a disproportionally high share of idiots, even compared to other government agencies."

"But you don't look like an agent," Jen said.

"Yeah, when you look as young as I do, all the FBI wants you to do is sex crimes. I got tired of meeting middle age men in video chat rooms pretending to be a fifteen year old. It started to screw with my dating life. Chasing fake werewolves is actually less stressful. In this role, I can dress any way I want. Since no one actually acknowledges the existence of our little group, it's hard to enforce dress standards. In the government, if it's written down, it's subject to a freedom of information request. If it's not written down, it doesn't exist."

Max turned pale as he realized something. He looked at Lizard and asked, "So you've actually shot someone with that gun you pointed at me?"

"I've killed a number of people with it." Lizard emphasized the word killed. "The Glock 21SF is an optional weapon for agents. I like it because the small grips fit my hand better and the forty-five caliber bullet gives it plenty of stopping power. That's important when a nut job who thinks they are a rabid werewolf comes running at you."

Max tried to get his manhood back. "Where did 'Lizard' come from?" His tone indicated a challenge.

"My parents named me Elizabeth. In elementary school I hated my name and all the variations. Beth, Liz, Eli, 'weird anorexic girl', 'Goth witch', you name it. Someone called me Lizard and it stuck. It kind of fits my personality."

She narrowed her eyes and looked at Max. "So why do they call you Max? Is that some kind of small penis compensation nickname?"

Jen snorted, unable to contain her laughter.

"No, it's short for Maximillian," he said.

"So your parents knew it was going to be small when they named you?"

Max was getting upset. His voice rose. "My dick is not small!"

Jen was doubled over laughing now. The waiter shot them a funny look as he brought bread for the table.

"I'm just messing with you. Don't get your man thong in a wad, and for that you can quit the special agent Wong. You can go back to Lizard. I have a feeling that this case is going to be a challenge so let's be friends."

She paused. "In case you haven't noticed, my FBI evaluations said I need to work on my social skills. I'm still working on them."

Lizard turned to Jen. "So, were you two dating before the planes started going down or is this a high stress romance kind of thing?"

Jen spit Diet Coke across the table. Now it was her turn to look flustered. "We're not dating," she managed to dribble out while wiping her chin. Max looked surprised and then hurt.

Lizard changed the subject. "Since we're sharing life stories, how did a white boy like you end up as a Mayan expert?"

Max sat back. "My father was Mexican. He came to the U.S. for college and returned home with a pale, red-headed, Irish-American bride. My grandmother was relieved that at least she was Catholic. The Gutierrez family ran a small bank near Mexico City and my father went to work in the bank. A few years later my parents had a bright white, red-headed Mexican baby. I spent eight years growing up in Mexico, learning Spanish in school and speaking both Spanish and English at home. My grandfather would regale me with stories of old Mexico, of the Aztec and the Maya.

The year I turned nine, there was a wave of bank consolidations in Mexico. Big banks were buying small ones and the family sold their little bank. My father took a job with a big U.S. bank in North Carolina. It was tough being a little red headed spic in the Deep South. It drew me closer to my Mexican roots, so I chased my heritage via books. In the process, I fell in love with both the Maya and books. Since I was never into banking, I decided to do what I love and try to make a living at it. At least, that's what I did until some crazy Mayan sky god started screwing everything up." He finished with a smile.

Their food arrived and the conversation inevitably drifted back to the crashes. After they had all agreed for the tenth time that the crashes didn't make any sense Lizard looked at Jen and Max.

"So just for a minute, what if there really isn't a rational explanation for all of this? Just speculating, what are the irrational options?"

Jennifer said, "You mean like a Mayan sky god had his book stolen and now he wants it back? That's crazy."

"Crazier than wings falling off airplanes in mid-flight?" Lizard asked. She turned to Max. "Crazier than multiple originals of an ancient Mayan codex turning up all over the place?"

Jen turned toward Lizard. "Do you really think that there is a supernatural element here?"

"Look, I don't know for sure. What I do know is that wings don't fall off airplanes and yet it keeps happening."

Max was still skeptical. "But what about the terrorists?"

"The government now believes it was terrorism," Lizard said. "I made some calls. The idiot that they caught trying to bring down a plane had a codex, but he didn't have any idea how to use it. He just jumped up and made a speech hoping the plane would crash, but he believed that the codex would crash the plane. A lot of other people are starting to believe it too. That's why panic is setting in. People know the idea is irrational, but they're afraid. Irrational fear quickly becomes panic."

Jen jumped in. "Also there was no evidence of terrorists or terrorism in the other crashes. We went through that first plane crash with a fine tooth comb. We were on it for weeks, nothing."

Wong cut to the chase. "Ok, so regardless of the cause, if we think the codex is bringing down planes, how do we prove it? Maybe it's not supernatural. Maybe there's a bizarre scientific explanation. If we can duplicate the crashes it may lead us to the cause."

"I like it," said Max.

"Wait, wait." Jen said. "We can't go around trying to crash planes, let alone succeeding."

Lizard ignored her. "So how do we test this?"

Jen started to protest again but stopped. She furrowed her brow in thought. "There may be a way. It's going to be expensive if we break his plane though."

Wong stared at her. "The reward is up to a million dollars for evidence leading to the cause of these crashes. Is it more expensive than that?"

"Ok, my dad's a pilot. He's got a small plane and we both know how to skydive. I may be able to convince him to let us try to crash his plane...but," she emphasized the word, "but if we actually crash his baby, he's going to expect us to buy him a new one."

# 11.

OMAR HAD READ ALL OF THE PRESS reports about Habib's capture. He didn't think that Habib would give them up, but he wasn't going to underestimate the FBI. The remaining three members of the fist of Allah were on the road now, headed east. Omar didn't have a specific destination in mind but he wanted to keep moving to stay ahead of the feds. He was driving the truck loaded with weapons, and Kaseem was sitting next to him. Mohammed was following in a worn out Toyota Corolla. They had stopped at a mall parking lot and switched plates with a random Corolla to make them harder to find.

The trio pulled off the highway. Omar and Kaseem pulled into a roadside motel. Mohammed continued on to different motel half a mile down the road. They hoped that this would make harder if anyone was looking for three men.

And hour later Mohammed showed up at Omar's room with takeout. It was time to plan their next move.

Omar stopped the video on his iPad. One of the passengers had been playing with their cell phone camera and managed to video most of Habib's incident. It was an instant YouTube sensation. The group had watched the video a dozen times so far. They winced every time they saw the ex-Marine slam Habib on to the floor of the plane, his head bouncing against a seat on the way down, and his arm bending at an odd angle.

Someone had cut just the part with Habib's head slamming into the floor into a Vine video and it ran in a continuous loop. Another user had remixed the video and overlaid the song Smack Down by Thousand Foot Krutch, timed to match Habib's head bouncing off the carpet. The world was laughing at them.

"Why didn't it work Omar?"

Omar thought it was ironic that the man named after the prophet was the one with doubts. He turned to Mohammed.

"It was not yet the will of Allah." He thought for a minute. "Perhaps Allah has more for us to do. We had a copy of the book, this codex. But we did not have the original. I think that Allah is telling us that we need the first codex to fulfill his plan."

"But surely the FBI has it locked up somewhere." This time it was Kaseem.

Omar stared hard at his little band. "That is our mission tonight. Find someone with access to the original. Find the expert who authenticated it, the investigator who found it or anyone else that we can use to get our hands on it."

The Fist of Allah fired up their laptops and iPads and did their best to overwhelm the budget hotel's weak Wi-Fi.

Four hours and countless Google searches later, they had some answers. Early the next morning they were back on the road with a destination in mind.

* * *

The next day, Jennifer couldn't get her father until after lunch. She hung up the phone and announced, "He's willing to do it. Dad spent a lot of years as an air traffic controller at Atlanta's Harts-field-Jackson International Airport. As he got older he moved to Atlanta's executive airport, Peachtree DeKalb or PDK. PDK is a lot less stressful for him. He knows what the stakes are if we don't solve these crashes, so he's willing to help. We just have to get to Atlanta."

"Drive or fly?" Wong asked.

"It's a toss-up. It's about a four hour drive to Atlanta. PDK is on the north side so it's a little shorter. If we fly commercial we'll end up south of the city and have to drive an hour or so back. It just depends on what flights we can get," was Jen's response.

"I say drive, who knows when the airports will get shut down. Closing down the airports is coming if we don't fix this," Wong said.

Jen and Max looked at each other and exchanged a little smirk. Max grinned and agreed. "Let's drive."

"You have a Harley and Jen didn't rent a car the last time we flew in, so I guess I'm driving." He pulled out his keys and they all headed downstairs. "Shotgun," Jen yelled.

"Oh hell no. I am not riding in that thing all the way to Atlanta," Wong said. She was standing on the curb staring at Max's bright blue little car. Jen giggled.

"Look it's this or nothing." Max wasn't happy when people ragged on his car.

"It's cute but what is it?" Wong finally asked.

"It's a MINI Cooper S and this little baby will do zero to sixty in 6.2 seconds. It's not cute, it's mean, and it's going to Atlanta." With that Max got in the driver's seat and slammed the door.

Jen opened the passenger door of the little sedan and pulled the front seat forward to let Wong in the back. "Shotgun remember?"

Wong scowled. "I have better idea. You two go to Atlanta. I'm going to find out more on the Raintrees and our terrorists. Whatever you do, don't lose the original codex. Don't let it out of your site. That may be the key." With that she headed to her Harley and rode off.

While Max drove, Jen used her iPad connected to a cellular network to go through the notes from crash survivors. Jen was particularly interested in the testimony of Linda Welsh. She was the one who had blamed the book publicly when the captain had miraculously saved Unified Air flight 3675.

Traffic was heavy because so many people were now refusing to fly. Max kept looking in the rear view mirror.

"What are you looking at?" Jen asked.

"I keep seeing a beat up Toyota in my mirror. I can't decide if he's following us or just going the same way we are."

Wong craned her neck and saw an old Corolla with faded gray paint two cars back.

"Pull over at the next exit and let's see if he follows. We could use a bathroom break anyway," she suggested.

Max took the next ramp and pulled into a monstrous gas station/convenience store combo. The MINI didn't need gas, even with the turbo the MINI sipped fuel. It wasn't quite as good as a hybrid, but then again, hybrids didn't really boast about zero to sixty numbers. Max topped off the tank anyway while Jen found the restroom and snacks. As Max replaced the gas pump handle he noticed a dingy, white panel truck pull in. He could swear that they had passed it a while back on the highway, but interstate travel was like that. This was a major road between Nashville and Atlanta. Most people drove within ten miles of the speed limit give or take, so you saw the same cars frequently. Max forgot about the truck and went inside to relieve himself.

Fully loaded with food and fuel they were off again. Max kept looking for the gray Toyota all the way to Atlanta. Sometimes he thought he saw it.

Other times he was convinced he was deluding himself. There were so many Corollas on the road that it was hard to tell. A few times he thought he saw the panel truck from the gas station too, but he dismissed those ideas. Who would be following them?

With the clogged roads, accidents were frequent. The trip took almost twice as long as normal. They reached Jennifer's father's place that night. He had an older three bedroom house on the northwest side of Atlanta. In their hurry to leave, the duo hadn't bothered to pack anything. They'd just hopped in the car and left. Jennifer drove back to her place for some clothes. Max, however, wasn't so lucky. Jennifer's dad was much shorter and wider than Max, so Max was stuck in a bathrobe for the evening while his clothes got washed.

Max watched Jen's dad as he made coffee. He was on the short side of average, maybe five feet seven. He had introduced himself as Hank and seemed nice enough. They all sat down with coffee.

Making small talk in nothing but a bathrobe was awkward, but Max did his best. "So Hank, Jennifer talks about you, but not about her mother. Is there a Mrs. Lynch?"

Hank looked sad. "We lost her to ovarian cancer when Jennifer was fourteen. It's a hell of lousy way to go. Nobody deserves to come down with that. I got to play both mother and father from then on. I think I pushed Jen toward airplanes."

"If you did, it was direction I was happy to go in," interjected Jen.

"Anyway," said Hank. "It's been a long time now. Speaking of airplanes, somebody fill me in on why we're going to try to crash my plane again?"

They took turns explaining the chain of events that had unfolded. Hank looked skeptical, but he agreed to take them up in the morning. Privately he thought the chances of crashing his plane by reading from an old book were pretty slim indeed.

* * *

Down the block, a gray Toyota with faded paint sat parked with the lights out. Mohammed was talking to Omar on a disposable cell phone.

"They are inside. Do you want to take them tonight?" he asked.

"No, they came here for a reason. Let's follow them tomorrow and see where they go. I will have Kaseem take your place in an hour. You've been following them all afternoon, and I can't have you falling asleep keeping watch."

Omar hung up. He and Kaseem were holed up in a budget motel about five miles down the road. They had found both Jennifer and Max's names in various news reports and had tracked down photos of each. Max's had come from the college website, Jennifer's from a "Women in Engineering" profile when she was at Georgia Tech. Omar believed that the man who authenticated the codex would be easier to find and could get access to the original. If he didn't have it, they would find some way to force him to get it.

The members of the Fist of Allah had driven all night to get to Nashville. As they finally found Max's bookstore, they saw both Max and Jen hop into the tiny blue car and drive off. Naturally, Omar followed them. The Fist of Allah had worked hard to keep from being spotted. He hoped they had succeeded.

* * *

The next day, everyone was up early. Hank played host making eggs and crispy bacon. He reminded Jennifer that he didn't get to do this enough.

"It would be nice if you would get busy working on some grandchildren for me," he teased.

"Wouldn't you like me to have a husband first?" she shot back smiling. Clearly this was a regular topic between them.

"Of course, but you don't seem to be moving very quickly on that one either. Take Max here."

Hank gestured toward Max with a spatula.

"He seems like a good catch. College professor, good looking. What's wrong with him?"

Hank turned to Max and watched him turn red. "You're not gay are ya'?"

Max spit his coffee across the kitchen surprise. After he wiped his mouth, he managed to get out "Uh, no. I'm definitely not gay."

Hank turned to Jen. "See you could marry him and give me grandchildren. Of course, he would have to get a bigger car."

The room erupted in laughter. Once breakfast was finished, they loaded into Hank's truck and headed to PDK.

# 12.

AT PDK, HANK KEPT HIS SINGLE ENGINE, four-seat Cessna 172 in a hangar he shared with a local flying club. He walked over to a table in the corner and started packing their parachutes. Jen went to help and Max followed.

As she helped her dad, Jen explained. "In college I got this weird idea that I really wanted to learn how to sky dive. So my father gave me lessons for my 21st birthday. We both did tandem jumps with an instructor and then moved on to solo jumps."

Hank explained, "I decided I couldn't live without her, so if she was determined to kill herself jumping out of a plane I was going to go with her."

When they were done, Hank preflighted the airplane. Jen led Max over to small office and showed him how to use the radio. Hank joined them after his preflight check.

"Ok, so what's the plan?" Max asked.

"Dad and I will go up in the plane with chutes on. He'll fly; I'll take the codex and try to crash the plane. You follow along on the radio. The terrorists couldn't figure out how to crash a plane so we may need some ideas."

"Where do you plan to test?"

Hank thought a minute. "There's a spot west of here where folks do some sky diving. Open fields, not many trees, still in radio range. I was thinking we should go there."

"I was thinking we should circle the field and shoot touch and goes. We'll test as we circle. That way if something happens we've at least got a shot at a safe landing," was Jennifer's reply.

Max looked worried. "Will you be high enough to jump out if something goes wrong?"

"I think we can arrange a long racetrack pattern, circle the field high. We'll tell the tower we're doing some tests." Hank had decided and that was enough for the group.

A few minutes later Hank and Jen were airborne. Flying in a Cessna 172 with a parachute strapped to their back was extremely uncomfortable. The alternative, being in a plane coming apart with no options was worse. Jen tested the radio link with Max while her dad monitored the tower frequency.

"Ok we're ready to go."

Jen opened the original codex. Nothing happened. She flipped through it, opened it up accordion style, flipped through it backwards. Nothing. The plane kept flying smooth and level.

She radioed Max. "Any ideas? I can't get anything to happen here."

"Try reading it," was Max's reply.

Jen started at the beginning. As before, she found that she understood the pictographs. She could indeed read the codex. Soon she was absorbed in it. Each page was rich with detail. She was again amazed at how much information was contained in a single set of images.

Still, several pages in, nothing had happened. They were still flying around in a lazy racetrack pattern. Jen put the book down to think. That's when it hit her. She keyed the radio.

"Max, do you remember what the Unified Express survivor said?"

Max thought for a minute and keyed the mike. "She was about halfway through. Something about death from above. Is that what you mean?"

"Yeah. I've got an idea." Jennifer turned to her father. "Take it up high and swing back for a long approach. Get ready to call 'Mayday'".

Jen flipped through the book to the middle. As they made the turn she skimmed as fast as she could. Jen stopped. She thought that she had found the passage, but she had another idea. Very slowly she interpreted the symbols as "Those who disturb the..."

The plane shook.

"What was that?" she asked.

"I'm not sure," her dad responded. "Probably just turbulence."

She went back to the book. "Those who disturb the sacred text of Q'uq'umatz shall suffer..." There was a loud crack and the plane plummeted downward. Hank fought for control. Jen looked out the window and saw that the right section of the wing was separating from the airplane's fuselage.

She turned to her dad and yelled, "Do you have it, or do we jump?"

He didn't answer. He was still wrestling with the control yoke.

"We're almost out of room. Land or Jump?" She reached for the door handle to bail out of the plane.

Slowly the nose came up. The wing was barely holding on, but it was still connected. Hank was doing everything he could to compensate.

"Mayday, Mayday." He called out their tail number. "We are declaring an emergency and asking for immediate landing priority."

Jen tightened her seat belt. Hank was still fighting the airplane to compensate for the partially severed wing. He was glad that he wasn't going to have to turn the plane. That would definitely be the end. Hank brought the plane in gently with slow movements. He was trying to get her down fast, but not so fast that the rest of the wing fell off.

Finally, the end of the runway was there. Desperate to get down, Hank rushed the landing. They came down hard. The front tire blew and the impact bent the front fork. The plane hit hard enough to rip loose the rest of the right wing. The weight of the still attached left wing caused the plane to ground loop and swerve to the left, toward the grass at the end of the runway. The wing hit the ground as the blown front tire tore up the grass. The little Cessna flipped forward and landed upside down.

An airport fire engine roared down the runway with its siren screaming and air horn blaring. Max was already in Hank's truck right behind the fire truck. He pushed the old pickup faster and got there seconds ahead of the fire truck. Max ran to Jen's side and was relieved to see her struggling to crawl out her door. A fireman jumped off of the truck and pulled Hank from the pilot's seat. Other firemen were starting to hose down the plane to prevent a fire.

Once Jen was clear, Max reached in and grabbed the codex. As he pulled his head out, he looked across the airfield. Next to the chain link fence at the end of the field Max saw a faded gray Toyota. He squinted. It looked like there was someone in the car. A fireman grabbed him and dragged him away. By the time he was free to look back, the Toyota was gone.

Hank's plane was a total loss. Police arrived to take statements. It looked like they were going to lose the whole day to answering questions about the crash until Hank pulled out his FAA card. He knew everyone at PDK and it helped that they vouched for him. Jen pulled out her NTSB credentials. Max's American Booksellers Association card wouldn't do him any good here so he sat down and shut up.

Finally, a police lieutenant looked at Jen and said, "Well, plane crashes belong to the NTSB and you're already here, so I guess you know what crashed the plane." He gave her a hard look. "You'll let us know if there is anything we need to know about this crash right?"

She let the words hang for a minute and just nodded. There was no way that she was going to tell them what crashed this airplane.

Hank made arrangements to have the parts hauled to the hangar for the insurance company to look at. Jen pulled out her phone and called Lizard.

\* \* \*

Omar had been behind the wheel of the Toyota when the Cessna crashed. So the government has figured out how to crash planes, he mused. He could swear that the nerdy looking one had stared straight at him. Omar needed a new plan. He wanted the codex, and he wanted to know how to use it. They had already sacrificed Habib to this mission. He didn't have many more men to give. He didn't want the codex disappearing into FBI headquarters. An idea hit him. The start of a new plan.

Omar pulled off the road and called a quiet contact that he had at Al Jazeera, the Islamic news agency. After a short conversation, he pulled up and reviewed the photos he had taken from the Cessna crash. There was the NTSB agent. He had several shots showing Max pulling the codex from the crash. Everything went to an anonymous online account that his contact had access to. They would need to keep a close eye on this group.

* * *

Back at her father's house, Jen's cell phone rang. It was her supervisor, Ed Rollins.

"Jen, they want you down at the office in Atlanta. Now." He emphasized the last word.

"Ok. What for?" she asked.

"One, NTSB agents investigate crashes, they don't get involved in them and they sure as hell don't cause them. Two, Al Jazeera is using your little stunt to claim that the federal government is behind these crashes. It's all over the TV news and the internet. Everyone is going nuts right now. They want someone's head and it may be yours."

"Shit," was her first response. "I'll be there in an hour."

* * *

The NTSB office that Jen was officially attached to is in the Atlanta Federal Center in downtown Atlanta. Ed intercepted her as she walked in and steered her into a large conference room. The room was full and several separate arguments were underway at the same time. People were seated at the table and around the periphery of the room. Ed motioned to the only open seat at the table and stood in the back corner.

Jen sat down. Her nerves were on edge. A sharp eyed man in well-tailored suit cut off his argument and turned to her. The gray at his temples, and the way the room quieted when he turned, were clear indicators of his seniority. The man's blue eyes narrowed and a sneer crossed his face. Jen shivered involuntarily as her thoughts turned to weasels.

"Welcome Agent Lynch," he started. "I'm Supervisory Special Agent Graham and I'm in charge of the FBI investigation into these airplane crashes." He emphasized the letters 'FBI'. "Al Jazeera has made a public claim that the federal government is taking down these aircraft and they have pointed the finger at you as proof."

"Agent Graham, I can assure you that I had nothing to do with these crashes."

"But you were the one to find a pristine codex in the middle of a field full of airplane debris. You were the one who identified it as a signature. Now you've been implicated in a crash involving a small plane." His tone turned ominous. "I want you to tell me everything you know about these crashes right now. Based on what I hear, I will decide whether you walk out of this room in handcuffs or not."

Jen shrugged and told him everything.

When she was done, the room was silent. Supervisory Special Agent Graham just stared at her. Finally he said, "That is the stupidest fucking thing I've ever heard. Reading from a book causes planes to crash? You expect us to believe that crap? I should have known that whack job Wong was involved. Lynch pointed at her. As of now, you are suspended. This is an FBI investigation and you're running around with a key piece of evidence, the codex from the first crash. That stupid book expert is out too. As for Wong, well, I will deal with her."

Jen wasn't so easily cowed. "SSA Graham, you may or may not have the authority to suspend me, but either way, I'm an agent of the NTSB. I have not broken the chain of evidence on the codex, and as I understand it, the President asked Agent Wong to look into this. If you've met Agent Wong, I think you know that you're going to have trouble dealing with her."

SSA Graham went from angry to completely out of control. His faced turned red. Spittle flew from his mouth. "I will handle the President and Wong. I will also handle this investigation and, since you are so concerned with the chain of evidence, where is the codex?"

"Agent Wong has it," she lied.

"You will go to Agent Wong, retrieve the codex, and bring it back here immediately. Is that clear?"

"Yes, sir."

On the way home, Jen called Wong.

"How did it go?" Wong asked.

"Bad. I'm suspended, Max is out, SSA Graham is gunning for you, and I'm supposed to return our original codex. Oh and I almost died this morning in a plane crash."

"Wait, do you mean SSA Sydney Graham?"

"Yeah. We met once before at a briefing, but we're really not on a first name basis. His ego doesn't leave room for friends."

"Well we're not giving back the codex. I'm at your dad's house. By the time you get here we'll try to have a plan."

\* \* \*

In the White House the President wasn't taking the news well either.

"Goddammit! Why is it that even with Wong barely attached to this I get covered in the stink of bad press?"

His chief of staff knew better than to tell the President that he had been against using the Lizard.

"Do want me to pull her off?" he asked. "The director of the FBI is screaming for her head."

"Hell no. As bizarre as it seems, she actually appears to have made some progress. The FBI performs better with a little competition. Just keep the director from mentioning Wong on camera. Do a press conference. Brush off the claims as wild conspiracy theories. They come from Al Jazeera for Christ's sake and we've got an attempted terrorist in custody. Leak the idea that Al Jazeera is trying to distract people from the Muslim terrorist caught in the act of trying to take down a plane. Oh, and tell Wong to find the fucking problem and fix it!"

* * *

Wong sat down with Max while they waited for Jen. Lizard arrived a few minutes after Jen left and Max filled her in on their busy day.

"You're going to have to run," she said. "But we need to figure out where. I need you to suspend disbelief for just a few minutes and go into crazy land with me. If we're going to save Jen's career and the airline industry I need your help. "

"Ok. Today's little incident almost has me convinced. Let's go to crazy town."

"Say that this is the book of this sky god, cuckoo for Cocoa Puffs or whatever his name is."

"Q'uq'umatz," Max interrupted.

"Yeah whatever. Some family skips Disney World to play in the ruins. They pick up the book and make off with it. They probably don't know what they have. Old cuckoo mats wants his book back. He's the sky god so he starts crashing planes. Copies of the book keep showing up. He's trying to punish us for stealing the book. He's telling us something. What is it?"

"He wants his codex back?"

"He wants his codex back." It was a statement not a question. "How do we give it back to him?"

"You know, we've been through the codex repeatedly, but with all the running around we've really only read all the way through it from beginning to end once. Maybe there is something in there about returning the book."

"But where do we return it to?"

"Calakmul." Max's tone radiated certainty. "The first plane to crash left from Cancun. Everybody did the tourist thing, but that one family, ah, the Raintrees, right? They went to Calakmul. Everybody else we've looked at didn't go near Mayan ruins. If we're going to run, we have to go to Mexico. We can read the codex on the way from beginning to end. We'll see if there is some instruction to return it."

The front door flew open. Wong's gun came out as Jen ran through the door. The words came out between ragged breaths.

"There's been a gray Toyota trailing me since I left Federal Plaza. Guy inside looks Middle Eastern. Also there's an unmarked truck parked down the street."

"Unmarked like surveillance van unmarked?" Wong asked.

"No. Like a small moving truck, dirty white, illegible, faded lettering on the side. Two guys sitting in the cab."

Wong started barking orders.

"Max, grab the codex. Both of you grab whatever stuff you have. We're out of here."

"Where's my dad?"

"He ran to the store...in his truck. Damn it. Now we have to go cross country in the MINI. Call or text him later Jen. We're out of time."

They ran for the garage and threw their stuff in the MINI. As Max backed out, Wong turned her head and saw three men running at them with rifles in their hands.

"Max, we've got company, step on it!"

Max floored the MINI triggering its over boost mode and adding an extra twenty horsepower for a short stretch. The car shot down the street. In his mirror, Max saw flashes. They were shooting at them.

# 13.

OMAR SWORE AT THE RAPIDLY accelerating blue car. His men had not practiced enough with their weapons. Dark skinned men shooting AK-47s at the local rifle range might arouse suspicion, so they weren't prepared for the recoil.

"Follow them!"

Omar ran for the truck. Mohammed headed back to the Toyota.

The blue MINI roared through traffic. Max raced through the gears and pushed the MINI like the little race car that it wanted to be. In the back, Lizard compensated for the way Max was weaving through traffic. She buckled in and held on to both "oh shit" bars in the back seat.

Riding shotgun, Jen had both hands wrapped around the handle above the door to avoid ending up in Max's lap. Max swerved right. As Jen bumped up against the window she asked, "Who were those guys?"

"Friends of our arrested terrorist," grunted Lizard as Max took another sharp turn. "Max, turn up here. Get off this road, we need to lose them."

Max turned right, then made a series of zigzag turns. They ended up in an industrial area parked behind a row of warehouses with storefronts on the other side.

Max was sitting in the driver's seat shaking. "What do we do now?" he asked.

Jen's faced tightened as she set her jaw. "We return the codex to Calakmul."

"Lizard and I were talking about that when you walked in. We still don't know what to do with it when we get there," protested Max.

He got a warm smile from Jen. "I'm sure you'll figure it out."

It was Lizard's turn. "Since we're not giving SSA Graham the codex, the FBI is going to raise a stink. They are going to be looking for us, along with the guys who just shot at us. That's a lot of people to run from. We should think about driving straight through, as much as we can."

"Can you keep the FBI off of us?" asked Max.

Lizard shook her head. "Probably not. I think I can keep us from going to prison, but if the FBI wants to find us they can. If they catch us, they can make our lives uncomfortable for a very long time, even without a conviction. We need to hit a bank and get as much cash as we can before they really start looking."

"Should we change cars?" Jen asked. "After all, the terrorists know what it looks like?"

Max looked hurt, but Lizard shook her head again.

"No. The FBI doesn't know about this car yet. It's Max's, not yours. It will take them a little while to find it. We can't go back to your dad's house with the terrorists around and we can't rent anything. The rental companies have tracking mechanisms on their cars to prevent theft. That reminds me, we need to dump our cell phones and get prepaid phones. Get moving Max, we've got a lot to do before we run."

* * *

Omar cursed when they lost the little blue car. He sent Mohammad in the Toyota to the top floor of a parking deck hoping to get a glimpse of MINI blue on the main street below.

Kaseem and Omar parked the truck at the top of an overpass. Kaseem raised the hood and pretended to work on the engine while looking one direction. From the cab, Omar looked the other way.

It was Mohammed who found them. He caught a glimpse of blue pulling into the back parking lot of a small bank branch.

Omar and Kaseem took off as soon as they got the call. "Dump the Toyota and find another car, but don't lose them," Omar insisted.

Mohammed was panicking. "Allah will provide." He kept telling himself. Just then a middle aged woman walked down the row he was parked in. She was dressed professionally, maybe a secretary Mohammed thought.

Sarah Duckworth actually managed a small team of mortgage brokers. She had come in late after fighting to get her kids up for school and now she had to leave early for a stupid dentist appointment. This was not her day for getting things done.

Sarah hit the clicker to unlock her Toyota minivan. It wasn't that old, but kids are rough on cars and she was ready for something new.

The kids are getting older. Maybe I'll get a Lexus instead of a minivan next time, was her last thought before a dark haired man with a short beard pointed a large pistol at her head. She opened her mouth to scream and got smacked in the face with the barrel for her efforts.

"T-t-t-take whatever you want," she stammered, blood pouring from her mouth and nose. The man grabbed her keys from her hand and motioned for her to walk.

Once she was behind the Toyota, Mohammed opened the trunk. "Lean in," he said.

"Please don't shoot me. I have children." She was crying now.

Mohammed hit her on the head as hard as he could. She slumped over the threshold of the trunk. Mohammed heaved her in and slammed the lid down. He didn't want the attention that a gunshot would attract, and he hoped that they would be long gone by the time she was found.

* * *

Jen and Max both used a large national bank so the little group headed for the closest branch. Banks carry less and less real cash these days and large cash transactions require paperwork so they each walked out with about five thousand dollars in mostly hundred dollar bills.

Lizard made everyone dump their cell phones in the dumpster behind the bank. The FBI would eventually find the cash transactions, they might as well try to end the trail there.

After that it was three miles to a strip mall that had a store that sold disposable phones. Max watched for a gray Corolla the whole way, but everything looked clear.

* * *

Mohammed caught up with Omar and Kaseem. They had followed the MINI and then driven past the strip mall to a McDonalds down the street. Kaseem walked out to watch the MINI while Omar and Mohammed transferred crates of weapons from the truck to the minivan. They lifted the truck's door just enough to slide the crates out. The group would have to abandon much of their stash so they concentrated on rifles, pistols, and ammunition. They managed to squeeze in two cases of rocket propelled grenades just in case.

When they were done, Omar locked the truck and switched the license plate on the Toyota minivan with a car parked in the back. Mohammed had described how he got the minivan and they needed to sanitize it any way they could.

* * *

The bank and the cell phones had taken longer than Lizard wanted. As they loaded back into the car, Wong said, "Take me to a MARTA station. I'm not going with you. I'm going to try to clear your way." Max and Jennifer protested, but Wong would not change her mind. "I can better hold off the FBI if I'm not on the road." They took her to the nearest station for Atlanta's MARTA train. As she was leaving, Wong leaned in the window. "Head toward Calakmul. Remember, we're the only ones who know where you are going. They have a whole country to search. Call me with your plan and I'll try to steer them the wrong way." With that, Wong was gone.

Atlanta traffic was heavy as they headed south on I-285 and then west on I-85. They would connect with I-65 in Montgomery and I-10 in New Orleans to take them west.

* * *

In the Atlanta Federal Building, SSA Graham looked at his watch then turned to another agent. "Bring me that NTSB guy. Ed what's his name."

Ed walked in a few minutes later and Graham started in on him.

"Your girl is late. All she had to do was drive home, grab this codex thing, and drive back. Two hours, three tops, even in Atlanta traffic. You said I could trust her. You said I didn't need to send an agent with her. She'll come right back you said. Now she's running. I blame you and I blame agent Wong, but it doesn't matter. Your girl is in the wind with my evidence."

"Jennifer Lynch is good agent and a good crash investigator. She's a by the book type of investigator. She isn't running," Ed responded.

"She's running. Call her, find her. If she isn't here in two hours we'll find her."

Ed walked into the hall and called Jen again. He'd left a dozen messages so far. "Jen you have to call me. If you're not here in two hours the FBI is coming for you. Call me now."

In the dumpster, Jen's cell phone recorded the call. She never got the message.

Two hours later Graham put the word out to all police agencies. Find and detain Jennifer Lynch, Maximilian Gutierrez, and Agent Elizabeth "Lizard" Wong.

* * *

Hours later Max and Jen raced southwest on I-65. Jennifer was driving now. Max's bulk was wedged in the passenger seat. He was studying the codex trying to figure out how to return it.

"There really isn't anything in here about returning the codex," Max lamented. "Calakmul is about three hundred miles southwest of Cancun. We know that a volcano just became active in that area. Now that I seem to have accepted that a Mayan sky god is crashing airplanes over his missing sacred codex it's tough to call a volcano near the site a coincidence. God, I've become a conspiracy nut." Max shook his head.

"Quit complaining and apply your newfound conspiracy knowledge to how we're going to get to Calakmul. We're fugitives remember?"

"Yeah, but where should we be going to? Calakmul or the volcano? In all the movies they always throw precious things into volcanos."

Jen shook her head. "We're not Hobbits and this isn't a ring. I say Calakmul first."

"OK. Google maps says the most direct driving route to Calakmul is about 45 hours, with a good chunk of that driving through Mexico. Given the on-going drug violence in Mexico, I'm not sure that's the best idea. There will be a lot of cops too and there aren't many alternative routes. Even if we flew to Cancun, it's still like a seven hour drive."

"Well we can't fly, the airlines are mostly grounded, and we'd be caught for sure if we tried to get on a plane. See if a there's a ferry or a boat or something."

\* \* \*

SSA Graham was running the investigation out of Atlanta for now. Lynch was on the run. He assumed Gutierrez was with her. Wong had disappeared. That made him nervous.

One of Graham's better agents rushed in holding a piece of paper. "Boss we caught a break. Atlanta P.D. took a report from a woman whose minivan was carjacked in a parking garage on the northwest side. She was knocked out and locked in the trunk of a beat up Toyota. Once she came to she kept banging and yelling until someone heard her and called the police."

"You don't think it was Lynch and Gutierrez?"

"No, the carjacker was dark skinned and he had a beard. Stay with me for a second. Later, the police were called to search a suspicious truck in a McDonald's parking lot a couple of miles away. They found a cache of weapons and not light stuff, AK's, RPG's, a fifty caliber machine gun and lots of ammo. Both the truck and the car had stolen plates. We traced the VIN numbers back to East St. Louis, Ill."

He paused dramatically.

"Do you remember who else was recently from East St. Louis?"

"Our little wannabe terrorist nugget Habib."

"Exactly. We have security video from the McDonalds. The woman has tentatively identified one of the guys from the video as her carjacker. We're working on ID's. We should have names on these guys in a couple of hours. "

"Bingo. The terrorists are in town. But why switch cars and leave half their stuff behind?" Graham asked.

"They made the switch in broad daylight. We don't know why they took the woman's minivan, but we think that they couldn't carry everything. Also, we have reports of shots fired near Lynch's father's house. We're assuming it's related for now."

"Ok, I want everyone in this city, and I mean everyone from the meter maid to the mayor, looking for these guys. That minivan is priority one."

Suddenly Graham was feeling good about running this out of Atlanta. The terrorists were here and he was going to catch them.

# 14.

JEN AND MAX HAD BEEN ON THE road for
five hours. Traffic out of Atlanta had slowed
them down a little, and they were still three
hours from New Orleans. The events of the
day had been exhausting. There had been no sign of
the gray Toyota or the dirty white truck.

Max was behind the wheel again. Jen was arguing
that they were going to need to stop.

"Max, so far today, just today, I've been in an airplane crash, suspended from work, shot at and now
I'm a fugitive from the FBI. We have to find a place
to hide out for the night."

"Look, I'm good. I can drive all night. Lay back
and relax."

As the words came out of his mouth a Mississippi State Trooper raced out of the bushes behind them with lights flashing and siren blaring. Max jerked involuntarily and started to pull over.

"No!" Jen yelled and grabbed the wheel to push them back on to the road. The trooper raced by in the left lane and pulled over a Dodge Charger about a mile later.

Max and Jen were both breathing hard.

"Sorry," Max started. "It was a reflex. Maybe I'm not as good at this fugitive from the law thing as I think I am. We're like three hours from New Orleans. We'll find a place near there to get some sleep and new clothes and then we'll hit the road again."

\* \* \*

Behind Jen and Max, the trooper had scared Omar too. The Fist of Allah was staying back and following the codex. Omar wanted the codex, but he needed to know how to use it. He wasn't ready to kill them both yet. The attack at the house had been a mistake, but he was hoping to catch them inside. The blue car coming out of the garage had surprised them and they'd reacted...badly. He asked Allah for patience.

The trooper's siren had woken up Mohammed. Thank Allah that he didn't start shooting, thought Omar.

"It will be harder to follow them if they go into New Orleans," Mohammed observed. He is right, thought Omar. This minivan is extremely inconspicuous, but a sharp move in traffic could expose them.

"We need to take them before New Orleans," Omar agreed.

\* \* \*

About an hour outside of New Orleans Max stretched behind the wheel. They were still outside the suburbs. It was nearing midnight and the light traffic made the road seem very dark.

In his mirror, a set of headlights was catching up to them. Max moved right to let them pass. The headlights materialized into a minivan that pulled into his blind spot and sat there.

"Idiot," Max mumbled.

Jen stirred. "Huh, what?"

"Just some moron who acted like he wanted to pass and is now just sitting there." Max pushed the accelerator to move ahead.

"Max lookout!" Jen screamed as she looked back.

Max stomped on the gas as the minivan swerved right trying to hit them. His MINI Cooper was short enough that the van missed and almost drove off the road. Jen caught a glimpse of the driver and recognized him. The last time she had seen him he had been firing an assault rifle at them in front of her dad's house.

"It's the terrorists Max. Go, go!"

The minivan regained the road and took off after them. Max saw red flashes in the mirror. Someone was leaning out the passenger window shooting at them. Max swerved the MINI to make them a tougher target.

There was an exit up ahead. Max moved to the left lane and slowed down slightly.

"Max, what are you doing?" Jen's tone was low. She sounded scared.

"Hold on and get down," he said as he flipped up the armrest. "This is going to be close."

The minivan was behind them and they were almost past the exit when Max jerked the wheel right and pulled the hand brake. The MINI responded instantly by slewing right; tires and brakes smoking. The terrorist van shot past still firing.

Max had almost cut it too close. Bullets ricocheted off the pavement around them as they bounced through the grassy median at the edge of the exit and up the exit ramp.

Max went right at the top of the exit ramp and kept the accelerator down.

"Shit," he blurted out looking at the dashboard. "They hit at least one tire." Max cycled through the computer screen in the center. "They got the rear tire on the driver's side."

"Can we put on a spare?"

"The MINI is too small for a spare. The good news is that MINIs come with run flats. The tire will lose air, but it won't go completely flat. If we're careful we can make into New Orleans, but we need to figure out what to do when we get there."

Jen pulled out her phone and called Wong's disposable cell. Wong answered on the first ring. Jen explained their situation.

Wong sounded thoughtful. "We need to get you to Calakmul as fast as possible. Driving there isn't going to work. It will take too long and there are too many variables. Plus you don't have passports. Last time I checked, Mexico was still another country and they are enforcing passport rules to cut down on drug running. Lots of people go back and forth illegally, but you probably want to avoid a Mexican jail. In fact, if you have a choice, take an American jail."

"We're getting shot at and you're being a smart ass," raged Jen.

"I've got an idea. Try to find a place to hold up tonight. Tomorrow, get to the Venice docks at sunrise. I think I know a way, but I need to call some people."

Jen had a piece of paper out. She scrawled "Venice docks, sunrise."

"Wait, Venice?"

"Yeah. New Orleans isn't right on the Gulf of Mexico. Deepwater stuff goes out of Venice. It's about an hour and half south. Do we have a plan yet for what happens in Mexico?" Wong asked.

Jen shook her head. "We're leaning toward Calakmul, but we think the new volcano is significant too."

"I've been through everything again. I still think the Raintrees are the key. They stayed at the Hotel Puerta Calakmul. I think we need to start there."

Jen scribbled "Hotel Puerta Calakmul" on her sheet.

"Hide the car, get some food and some sleep. I'll text you the dock number once I have it pinned down. Trust me." With that Wong hung up.

Max got them back on track, headed toward Venice instead of New Orleans. He had to slow down to compensate for the tire. They found a low end motel off the highway with a courtyard that let them hide the MINI from the street.

The room looked clean enough. Jen took a shower and wrapped herself in a towel. While Max was in the shower she washed her clothes out in the sink. They really needed to learn to pack some clothes before running off on these crazy quests.

Max and Jen ended up with a single, king-sized bed in their room. The desk clerk had assumed that they were a couple and Max was afraid that asking for two beds would look suspicious. Now with both of them sitting on the edge of the bed wearing nothing but towels, it was just awkward.

Max broke the tension with an idea. "Look, we need sleep. Sunrise isn't that far off. You sleep under the sheet. I'll sleep on top of the sheet and under the um...nasty comforter. "

Jen laughed and shyly slipped off her towel. "Or you could join me under the covers."

# 15.

JEN AND MAX DIDN'T SLEEP AS MUCH AS
they would have liked, but they did wake up
feeling better. The stress of the last couple of
days still took its toll. They were up at sunrise,
but moving slowly. Their clothes were stiff from air
drying, but with terrorists and the FBI on their tail
they didn't have too many options.

Jen checked her texts. She found one from Lizard
that read "Dock 67 Venice Marina." Outside, the
MINI looked worse in the light. There were half a
dozen bullet holes in the rear fender on the driver's
side. At least three had gone all the way through and
created exit holes on the passenger side. The run flat

capability seemed to be intact on the tire that had been hit. Max hoped it would hold.

Max drove slowly, trying not to draw attention. The dock area was confusing and several times they got lost. When Max finally pulled up to dock 67 it was more than an hour past sunrise. As he parked, they saw a large sport fishing boat. The boat was sleek with a large center cabin, an open rear cockpit for fishing and a large flying bridge for spotting fish while steering.

Max read the sign. "Missy Lee, sixty-two foot Striker. Inshore and offshore fishing charters. Ask for Captain Jack." They walked down the dock.

"Can I help you folks?"

Jen looked around for the voice.

"Up here."

Max and Jen looked up. A heavy set bald man was up on the boat's flying bridge.

"We're here for a boat," Jen told him.

"Huh. Only charter I had for today was supposed to be here at sunrise. You guys are at least an hour past that so it couldn't be you."

"Lizard sent us."

"The only Lizard I know works for Homeland Security and she's a pretty scary lady. Usually when she tells people to be somewhere they show up on time."

Jen had reached her limit. "Look buddy, we've had a hell of a couple days. I agree, Wong is scary so are you gonna take us out or do I have to call her?"

The captain climbed down from the flying bridge. He stepped on to the dock and got uncomfortably close to Jennifer.

When he spoke, his voice was low, not much above a whisper.

"What's the name of the family that Wong thinks is the key to this mess?"

"Raintree," she whispered back.

It was a reflex answer. She didn't pause, didn't stop to think, and didn't have to look at notes.

"Get your stuff and get on board as fast as you can. You guys are really late. There's a storm brewing and we've got a small window of opportunity."

They grabbed the files and the codex. There really wasn't much else to take.

Once on board, the captain ushered them into the cabin.

"You two have a lot of people looking for you. It would be better if you stayed inside until we're at sea."

Max looked out the open cabin door.

"Is it safe to leave my car out there?"

The captain looked back at the bullet ridden MINI.

"Son, it looks like you're better off without it."

With that the captain was gone. A few minutes later they heard the engines start and the boat pulled away from the dock. Max and Jen looked out the tinted windows as first the harbor, then the river, and finally the tidal marshes slipped past them.

Once they were in the open ocean, the captain came in.

"Ok, autopilot's set. It's about eighteen hours to Mexico if the weather holds. There's a tropical storm trying to form and if it hits us, it's going to be bad. I assume that you're Max and Jen. I'm Captain Jack."

"Like the pirate?" Max was grinning.

"No, not like the fucking pirate," Jack scowled. "I was Captain Jack long before that poof Johnny Depp was."

"Sorry, I'm sure you've heard that before," Jen said as she shot Max a look. "We're still pretty worn out."

"Why don't you two get some rest while the weather is still good? The Missy Lee can handle the weather, but it may get really bumpy later."

* * *

It was noon when they found the car. Omar was sure that they had hit it last night. He wasn't expecting that crazy move the book expert had pulled. The

Fist of Allah had turned around illegally in the median as soon as they could. Omar had backtracked trying to find the MINI. They had looked all night. Sleep deprivation was starting to affect them too.

Omar was gambling that they wouldn't try to fix a car full of bullet holes. They had visited and called the airport, rental car lots, train stations, and bus stations. Nothing. Calling marina's looking for the car was their last hope. Mohammed covered himself as an upset car rental agent to avoid suspicion when making calls. They hit pay dirt with the Venice Marina.

Omar thought he was hallucinating when he found it. He rubbed his eyes twice to be sure, it was still there. The little blue MINI had bullet holes in the side. He left Kaseem behind the wheel while he checked out the car with Mohammed.

Omar thanked Allah for showing them where to find the car. He followed that with curses. There was no blood. His men had missed. They searched the car. Wedged in the space between the passenger seat and the door was a slip of paper. The hand writing was tough to read, like it had been written in a hurry on a rough road. Omar and Mohammed brought it back to the van to work it out. Ultimately they decided that it read "Venice docks, sunrise, Hotel Puerta Calakmul."

There was only one empty slip near the car. Dock 67. The Missy Lee.

Omar motioned to Mohammed. "Get out your smartphone. Find this Hotel Puerta Calakmul."

Omar wandered down the line of boats. He was looking for something. It would depend on where the resort was, but Omar was sure now that they had left by water. A dozen or so slips down, he found a possibility.

"Hello," he called out. A man detached himself from a small group three slips down and came over.

"Howdy. What can I do for you?"

"This is a very fine boat."

"Yes she is. The Terminator is a fifty-foot Nor Tech catamaran. She'll do a hundred and fifty miles an hour in calm seas."

"With that kind of speed she must have a short range."

"Well, a stock boat will do a couple of hundred miles at cruising speed, but this boat has extended range fuel tanks. I got her at a police auction." His accent emphasized the "po" in police. "The previous owner tried to pay for her with a few illegal runs, if you know what I mean. She'll go six hundred miles on a tank at cruise speed."

"Is she available for rent?"

"Sure. There's some weather out farther, but we should be able to avoid that. Do you want to go out now?"

The boat captain had almost written off this day and now he was looking at a nice payday.

"Let me talk to my associates. One moment."

Omar wandered back to the minivan. Mohammed started talking first.

"The resort is in Mexico, three hundred miles from Cancun. It is near a large group of Mayan ruins. If the codex is Mayan, as the news reports say, they may be trying to find the source of its power."

"We are going to try to catch them. Pull the van up to that fast looking boat." Omar gestured toward the catamaran farther down. "We will need to travel light. One case of RPGs, one case of AK-47s, two boxes of ammunition and our pistols." He fingered the semi-automatic tucked into the back of his waistband.

Omar walked back to the boat. The small group of men was gone. The speedboat captain was the only one around.

"We would like to rent your boat for the afternoon."

The minivan pulled up blocking the view for half of the marina.

"Fantastic. Let me get the paperwork together."

Before he could turn away, Omar moved in close and pulled his pistol.

"I have all the paperwork you need right here. Put down your hands you stupid fool. You'll attract attention. Get in the boat."

Kaseem and Mohammed muscled a case each of AK-47's and RPG's into the small front cabin. Kaseem went back for the ammunition cases and they were off.

As they moved away from the dock, Omar took another look at his choice. The ocean racer had two long narrow cabins and a small cockpit that seated five. 'Seated' was a generous term thought Omar. The 'seats' were really bolsters designed to let riders take the shock of hard waves with their legs rather than their back.

"You'll never get away with this," said the captain. Omar smacked him on the side of the head with his pistol.

"You stupid Americans always say the same stupid things. No creativity. This is simple. We need to get to Mexico as quickly as possible without running out of fuel. If you take us there, we will get out and you can have your boat back. If you try anything, we will kill you, and right now I'm really in the mood to kill someone."

The boat owner reluctantly nodded in agreement.

"Go slowly until we hit the ocean. I don't want to attract attention."

"It's close to five hundred miles to Cancun. In an open boat with weather coming in. We'll break every bone in our bodies trying to make that happen."

"You'd better hope we don't. Mohammed, Kaseem, strap in."

\* \* \*

In Atlanta, the FBI investigation had stalled again. There had been no sign of the terrorists or the fugitives. Graham was throwing things around the conference room.

"I want these bastards Goddammit! We are close. Somebody find them for me!"

Graham's temper tantrums were legendary, but they were matched by his ability to catch criminals, so Washington tolerated his behavior. A rookie agent walked in. Graham threw a stapler at his head. The rookie ducked. Graham grunted.

"SSA Graham?" It wasn't really a question. The rookie was just nervous. "We have a lead."

"Well? Out with it."

"Police found Max Gutierrez's car by the waterfront in Venice, Louisiana, not far from New Orleans. It had bullet holes in it. They also found the carjacked minivan that we think the terrorists were using. There were cases of ammo, AK-47's and RPG's in the back. It looks like some weapons are missing, but it's pretty hard to tell."

"Any blood, bodies?"

"No blood and no bodies. Nothing indicates that anyone was hit, but we've found both of the cars and none of the people. No sign of the codex either."

Graham stood up and raised his voice.

"Ok everybody listen up. Load up the jet. We're moving this operation to New Orleans."

\* \* \*

On board the Missy Lee, the uneven pounding of the waves pitched Max out of his bunk. He woke up in a heap on the floor with Jen laughing at him. They carefully made their way out to the main salon, tripping twice along the way. Captain Jack was there at the controls.

Max and Jen flopped onto a couch as a wave tried to yank it out from under them.

"Jack, we were worried that you would be up on the flying bridge steering through all of this weather," Max commented.

"If you wanted an idiot for a captain you should have asked for my brother," he responded with a smile. "Did you get some rest?"

"Some, but what about you? Are you planning on being at the wheel the whole way?"

"I got a little nap in earlier when I could still use the autopilot. It's on now, but I have to keep over-riding it to get a smoother ride."

"This is a smooth ride?" Jen asked.

"It's going to get a lot rougher before we're through. The Missy Lee is designed to get to fishing areas fast, so she's got plenty of power and fuel to get us to Mexico. She's used to the open ocean so I think we'll be okay. Do me favor, though. Open that locker next to you and grab three life preservers."

"Seriously?"

"Yeah. It's just a precaution, but this storm is go-ing to get worse. It's organized into a tropical wave and may become a tropical storm. We really should-n't be out in this mess. Until we're safe, I want you to wear one of those. Toss me one too, and then toss me a beer."

They looked awkward sitting there in their or-ange life vests. Awkward enough that in a few minutes they were all laughing at each other.

Jack sipped his beer. "Oh yeah, one more thing. Reach into that locker over there." He pointed to Jen's right. "Pull out that waterproof pouch. I keep a few of those along for executives who can't bear to be separated from their iPhones, iPads, doo-dads...whatever. I picked the biggest, toughest ones I could find so they could use a device or protect it but not both." He chuckled at his own wit.

Jen reached in and pulled out a big Plexiglas box. The box was more than big enough for the codex. It had both a locking clip and a screw mechanism to keep the box waterproof. Jen retrieved the codex in its protective sleeve and slid the whole thing into the box. She secured the strap to her life vest and tied a second line to the box and around her waist. It would make the trip even more awkward, and she wasn't sure how she was going to go the bathroom, but she was determined not to lose the codex.

Max grabbed another box and stuffed it with everything else he could think of, cell phones, wallets, anything they might need that would fit.

"How are we doing on time?" Jen asked.

"It's going to be close. We want to get you on shore in the dark. The timetable was to get you there sometime between midnight and one AM. But you were late and this storm is slowing us down. Now, I'm hoping to just get you there before sunrise. You don't have passports so we're sneaking you in. The good news is that Missy Lee draws less than four feet of water so I can get you in close. The bad news is that the US and Mexico are working together to stop drug runners. We're going the wrong direction for the average drug boat, but we still need to avoid them.

* * *

There was no laughter aboard the Terminator. After they had been out about an hour Omar motioned for the captain to kill the throttles. He raised his gun at the captain. His eyes never left the man. Over the noise of the idling V8's, he yelled out.

"Mohammed, can you handle this?"

"Yes Omar. It will not be a problem. Allah Akbar!"

Omar pulled the trigger. The captain's head exploded. Blood sprayed over the side and his body slumped against the gunwale. Kaseem and Mohammed moved over and dumped his body over the side.

"Are you sure you can handle this Mohammed?"

"Yes. The GP coordinates are already set. This boat is simple, not much but throttles and steering."

Mohammed had been a mechanical engineer. Operating a motorboat was well within his capabilities. With Mohammed at the helm, the Fist of Allah was quickly pounding the waves toward Mexico.

Six hours later they were wet, cold, and sore with a very long trip still ahead of them.

# 16.

THE MISSY LEE APPROACHED THE Mexican coast. They had beaten sunrise, though it probably wouldn't have mattered. The air was heavy with gray ash from the volcano. Visibility was dramatically reduced as the newly-active volcano spewed debris across Mexico and into the United States. Rain and ash merged into a murky, soupy mist. The waves continued to pound the coast. The rough sea became more dangerous as the bottom rose up unevenly. Waves broke unexpectedly and Captain Jack fought to keep the boat from flipping.

The ash and the rain obscured any light from shore. It also made it hard for Jack to see the waves.

He caught a flash of light that he thought might be the beach, so he turned toward it. Too late he realized that it was the crest of a large wave. As the Missy Lee plunged in, the wave rolled the boat and washed over the top of the flying bridge. Max and Jen were thrown off of the couch.

As they came through the other side, the boat rotated past the centerline when a crossing wave caught them, flipping the Missy Lee completely over.

Captain Jack's head bounced against the window. Max and Jen were on the floor of the main cabin as water started pouring in through the rear doors. Max crawled through the water and grabbed Jack's life jacket. He yelled at Jen through the roaring water. "Open the door! I don't know if this boat will sink or float, but we can't stay in here."

To her credit, the Missy Lee didn't sink right away. Her all aluminum hull held and they bobbed and bounced just under the surface. Jen kept getting tossed away from the door and Max kept losing his grip on the captain. More water was coming in. They had seconds to get out.

Jen fixed her grip on the door as a wave flung the boat sideways. Jen hung on for dear life as the water, and the wave motion, flung her horizontally. The motion threw all of her weight against the handle and finally cracked the seal. The door at the rear of the main cabin popped open.

Max struggled to force Jack's lifeless form through the door. His bulky life jacket kept trying to float him past the opening. With his last breath, Max forced him down and out.

Jen's life jacket shot her to the surface. She opened her mouth to scream for Max and got a mouthful of saltwater for her trouble. Sputtering, she panicked. Max should be up by now. Finally she got it out, "MAAAAX."

Max popped up out of the depths still clutching Captain Jack. He tried to tow him to keep his head out of the water so he could breathe. Jack woke up when a wave smacked him in the face. Like his namesake, Captain Jack was hard to drown. The little group linked arms in a circle to try to stay together, hoping they were bobbing toward shore.

Dawn broke as a thin, gray line on the horizon. The wind finally slowed, but it would take days for the waves to settle. The rain continued. The survivors of the Missy Lee bobbed together. Suddenly, Jennifer cocked her head. The sea sounded different.

"Do you hear that?"

Max listened.

"Yeah. It's a roar. Like, like the surf. A beach!"

Captain Jack was still woozy. They suspected that he had a concussion. Slowly, with each of them holding one of Jack's arms, they towed him toward the sound of the surf.

As they got closer Jen realized that this wasn't going to be easy. The surf was running high and getting pounded onto a sandy beach hurts. They did their best to hold on to Jack and time their approach, but between their burden and the life jackets, they couldn't fight the surf. The little group was unceremoniously dumped into the shallows.

Jen crawled ashore. She saw Jack face down and crawled to him. With the last of her strength she flipped Jack over to keep him from drowning and flopped on her back. She felt a strong hand grab her and she watched, exhausted, as Max dragged her and Jack on to the beach.

They lay on the sand, vomiting sea water. Jen laid her head down on the wet sand. She could hear her breathing in her ears. She just wanted to lay there and sleep. She didn't want to have anything to do with any damned codex anymore. The codex. Jen sat up. There was still a rope tied to her life vest. She pulled on it and felt a tug. She pulled harder and the waterproof box with the codex came into view. Tears came to Jen's eyes. They were alive and they still had the codex. Okay, she still cared.

Jen was energized now. She heaved Max to his feet and together they supported the captain. Once off the beach they saw the lights of a hotel. Max and Jen dragged the captain into the lobby.

They showed up at the front desk looking like Jonah after he'd been vomited out the whale. They felt even worse. Jen was faltering. They dropped Captain Jack on to a sofa. Max started yelling. "Help, help our friend almost drowned.  Conseguir un medico. Conseguir un medico. Get a doctor!"

This was tourist Mexico and the storm and volcano had driven most of the tourists away. The staff came running to help anyone who still might tip. Max and Jen crashed into chairs. "Shouldn't we get him to a hospital?" worried Jen.

"This is Mexico. He's better off with a private doctor than in an ER. We're all dehydrated and need rest. Let's find another hotel down the beach to crash for a few hours. We don't want them to find us when someone starts asking questions about Captain Jack."

Jen looked concerned. "Will Jack be ok?"

"Yeah I'll make sure that they take good care of him. The bag with our wallets and cell phones made it too. We'll call Lizard when we get settled and have her make additional arrangements."

Max spoke quietly to the concierge in Spanish and handed him a wad of cash. A thousand would go a long way toward making sure that Jack was well cared for. In the chaos of people rushing around, they slipped out into the storm. Down the beach they found a Marriott and got a room at a significantly reduced rate. In their room they took a long, hot shower and then called Lizard.

"I'll deal with Jack, but you can't stay there. You have to go." Wong said after they had filled her in. "The terrorists hijacked an ocean racer and followed you. They aren't that far behind. You have to get to Hotel Puerta Calakmul by tonight."

Max wasn't convinced. "That's a six or seven hour drive, more like eight to ten in the dark, with bandits and who knows what else on the road."

Wong wouldn't back down. "Keep your room and find the concierge. Keep giving him cash until he finds someone to drive you. You two aren't in any shape to drive. Pay him enough to get a reliable driver, not enough to get you robbed on the road." With that, she hung up.

"Well that wasn't very helpful," Max said to no one in particular.

The concierge supplied his nephew and a well-worn Honda of indeterminate color for the small sum of a thousand dollars. Jen and Max tried to sleep, but the combination of rough roads and the Honda's worn out shocks made that all but impossible. They settled into a kind of rolling stupor for the next eight hours.

* * *

All of the members of the Fist of Allah were numb. They were freezing. Everything hurt, bone, muscle, joints, teeth, everything, but they were getting close. Omar hoped the ocean racer would hold together. The ash and rain made it seem like the sun had never risen. He was concentrating so hard that the searchlight surprised him. A Mexican navy patrol boat had found them and the light was blinding.

"Kaseem, RPG now."

The patrol boat was hailing them in Spanish and English. Mohammed angled the boat away. Tracer fire exploded ahead of the ocean racer, a clear sign to stop. The Mexican navy apparently didn't play games with suspected smugglers.

Omar lifted the RPG and rolled with the waves. For just a second the boat was stable and he pulled the trigger. The rocket propelled grenade ran true and exploded against the hull of the patrol boat.

# 17.

MAX AND JEN BUMPED ALONG IN THE old Honda. Five hours into the trip a particularly rough pothole temporarily jolted Max out of his stupor. Annoyed, he looked at their guide. The kid couldn't be more than fifteen years old, but he really wasn't a bad driver. The roads were unlighted and rough. The moon helped, but the interior of Mexico was still very dark. It didn't help that the Honda's shocks weren't in great shape either.

Their driver had been chatty when they started out. His name was Pedro. His father had been killed in the drug violence that plagued Mexico. Now he drove for his uncle and did odd jobs around the hotel. Max and Jen had been tight lipped, but they had warned the kid to watch out for cars behind them. They had no idea how far back the terrorists were.

As they rounded a bend, the Honda slammed to a stop. Two trucks blocked the road. The Honda's headlights illuminated men with guns. The sudden stop woke up Jen. Max was fully alert now.

"Don't worry, Mexican toll collectors," Pedro said as he opened the door and stepped out. He smiled. "I know what to do."

The kid got out and started yelling and gesturing, spewing an angry stream of Spanish. The driver's side window was down and Max could hear most of it. He translated for Jennifer.

"The kid's calling them all kinds of nasty names. He's telling them who he is and who his uncle is. Someone named Alejandro Salazar. Shit, Alejandro Salazar is the name of a Mexican drug lord. There was a 60 Minutes profile about him last year. The guy is bad news. Now he's telling them in explicit terms what his uncle will do to them. Oh, that's messed up. I'm not going to translate that."

Pedro gave the gunmen the finger and walked back to the Honda. Two gunmen rushed to move the trucks and let the Honda pass. As he got back in the car he asked, "How many men are chasing you?"

"Three," Jen answered automatically.

As the Honda pulled even with the trucks, Pedro slowed the car. He called out to lead gunmen. "There may be three men traveling through here later. They will be carrying a large amount of cash. Uncle Alejandro will be very unhappy if that cash is not collected as a toll."

Once they were out of sight of the gunmen, Jen asked, "I thought your uncle was a hotel concierge?"

Pedro's grin stretched from ear to ear as he looked back at them in the rear view mirror. "The concierge is my uncle, Uncle Miguel. He is the one who took me in after my father was killed in the drug wars. He wants nothing to do with the drugs. He thinks they are ruining Mexico. But my other uncle is Alejandro Salazar. He is part of the reason that my father was killed. I don't have much to do with him, but many people know that I'm his nephew. They know that it would be very bad to harm me. Uncle Alejandro controls this area and he feels bad about what happened to my father so he looks out for me. Sometimes I use his evil for good."

Max and Jen chuckled as the Honda continued its potholed journey to Calakmul.

\* \* \*

The next morning, Jen was curled up in bed with Max when Lizard shook her awake.

"C'mon wake up. We need to move."

Jen looked at her through mostly closed eyes. They'd arrived late that evening at Hotel Puerto Calakmul. Lizard was waiting for them with a doctor. He'd examined them, given them fluids, and prescribed bed rest. Jen had gotten some sleep, but she felt like she was still three weeks behind.

"The terrorists made it to Mexico."

What was Lizard saying?

"They're still following you. They shot it out with the Mexican navy earlier today. We have to assume that they know where you are going."

The fog in Jen's mind started to lift. "What time is it?"

"It's seven in the morning local time. I tracked down the guide that the Raintrees used. He told me that they hiked all over the site. They were kind of a pain. We have to get to Calakmul before the terrorists find us."

Once she had put everyone to bed the night before, Lizard had the hotel wash everyone's clothes. There hadn't been time to buy more. They dressed slowly. Max and Jen were still foggy, but they were moving.

In the lobby they met up with their driver. The hotel had supplied a van and it was waiting. As they slowly woke up on the ride to Calakmul, Max and Jen were overcome with hunger. Lizard kept handing them energy bars.

Max was whiny. "I don't want another energy bar. I want eggs with bacon, sausage, potatoes, a steak, some lobster." His voice trailed off.

Jen looked at him. "Sorry, you don't get that until after you save the world." Max chuckled, his mood lightening slightly.

Jen turned to Liz. "My brain is really foggy. Remind me again, how did you get here?"

"I flew here on a Mexican diplomatic flight. The President of Mexico owed me a favor. They had what they thought was a Chupacabra problem at one point. I helped resolve that little issue."

"So you flew here, in comfort, while we almost died multiple times?"

"Yes. The FBI can't touch me. I'm acting on direct orders of the President of the United States, and I wasn't being chased by terrorists. Besides, no one in their right mind would let you near a jet while you're carrying that codex." She pointed to Jen's new backpack where the codex was still in its waterproof case.

"Just having the codex won't crash a plane. You have to read it. We proved that."

"Would you risk your fifty-million dollar jet if someone brought you that crazy story? Look, you weren't going to make it driving across country with both the FBI and terrorists chasing you. Hell, you barely made it to New Orleans. Captain Jack knows how to drive a boat and we weren't expecting this to turn into a tropical storm." Lizard ignored Jen's glare. "It's time for the bigger picture. Where do we return the codex?"

Max finished stuffing down an energy bar before he spoke. "We think the volcano is related, but there's nothing necessarily volcanic in the codex. Spewing lava could be construed as death from above, but I'm not convinced. I keep coming back to Calakmul. That's where we think the codex was found. Plus, this isn't Lord of the Rings. If we toss the codex into a volcano it's going to burn. As a book seller, I have a philosophical problem with burning books. As a professor of Mayan studies, I don't want to be the guy who burned up the original codex only to see planes keep crashing. Plus, if it doesn't burn, none of us are going to be able to go in and get it back out. I say we go poke around Calakmul first."

Lizard looked at Jen. "And you?"

"I'm with Max. If we put the book someplace in Calakmul and nothing happens, we can get the book back. If we torch it, we're stuck."

"Which brings up my next two questions. How will we know when we did it right? Plus how do we keep the terrorists from just grabbing it back?"

Max and Jen looked stuck. They had been on the run for too long with too little sleep. Finally Max said, "I think we have to trust Q'uq'umatz. He's managed to tell us that he wants his codex back. Hopefully he'll tell us when he has it back and he'll protect it a little better this time. Then again, it took a couple of thousand years for someone to find it the first time. I'm willing to wait that long for someone to find it again."

The little group settled back as the bus bumped along toward Calakmul.

* * *

Omar guided his little band through the scrub to the road. They had beached the boat on a deserted stretch of sand. They couldn't carry the remaining RPG's, so they each settled for a pistol, an AK-47, and a couple of extra magazines.

Omar was ready to abandon stealth. Even in Mexico, it was hard to appear nonchalant carrying an assault rifle. The NTSB agent and the professor were up to something. He wasn't sure what it was, but he was worried that they were going to destroy the codex. There was no guarantee that they had survived the storm. If they died at sea, then losing the codex was Allah's will. Omar wouldn't believe they were dead until he had some proof.

A battered car came around the corner. Omar stepped out of the bushes and pointed his rifle at the car. With a squeal of breaks the battered Chevy screeched to a stop. The members of the Fist of Allah got in the car. Omar told the middle-aged woman who was driving to get out. The woman didn't have to be multilingual to understand.

Kaseem got behind the wheel. Mohammed had saved the route on his iPad and it had survived the trip. The tree of them alternated as they drove through night toward Hotel Puerta Calakmul.

They were switching drivers every two hours trying to stay awake. Mohammed was driving now and doing everything he could to catch up to their quarry. As he rounded a curve, he slammed on the brakes. Two pickup trucks blocked the road and a man with an AK-47 approached the car. For Omar, this was one more frustration. One more obstacle to overcome in their holy quest. He leaned in from the front passenger seat and whispered to Mohammed and Kaseem, "Kill them all."

Mohammed shot the man approaching the driver's side. Omar rolled out the passenger door and brought up his AK-47 firing on full auto. Kaseem did the same from the back seat on the left side. The banditos were expecting a car full of soft targets stuffed with money, not angry, assault rifle toting terrorists. The Fist of Allah mowed down the half dozen banditos, moved the trucks, and continued on. Omar felt better after the killings. He had spent a portion of his pent up rage. He would harness what he had left for those holding the codex.

* * *

Mohammed and Omar scouted the Hotel Puerta Calakmul. It was afternoon and they didn't have much time. Omar worked his way around front and found a bellman at the entrance. He guessed that the bell and desk staff would be more likely to speak English.

Omar approached the bellman. "Excuse me, I overslept and missed some of my friends this morning, a blond woman and a tall man. You don't know where they went do you?"

The bellman looked at Omar's disheveled appearance. "You don't know where your friends went?"

"We talked about a couple of different ruins. We didn't really decide." Omar slipped the bellman a twenty.

The bellman's mood brightened. Most tourists had fled when the volcano started spewing ash. Tips were becoming scarce. "I think I know the people of which you speak. They left on the hotel bus this morning."

The bellman waited. He'd done this dance before.

Omar sighed and pulled out another twenty. He didn't want to wave a gun around the front of the hotel. "And where did the bus go?"

"To the Mayan ruins at Calakmul."

Omar thanked him politely and asked for a map. Another twenty dollars later, and with a map in hand, he walked down the road to the car. "Omar tossed the map to Mohammed. They are at the ruins of Calakmul. Take us there."

\* \* \*

Lizard woke up Max and Jen as they approached the formerly lost city of Calakmul. They were so tired that neither the rutted road nor the excitement of solving the mystery of the codex could keep them awake through the drive. They climbed out of the bus and looked down on the site. It was massive. The codex could have come from any of the pyramids. It could have come from a pyramid still buried in the jungle.

As she looked over the site, Jen's heart sank. "I didn't think it would be this spread out. Where do we start?"

Max thought for a minute. "We need to think like the Raintrees, like eco-tourists. Mom, dad, a couple of kids. They get out here, where do they go?"

Lizard looked out, "The big white pyramid." All of the pyramids were made of a dark stone and covered in moss, but the one in the center was lighter. It was also the largest.

"Structure Two," Max said.

With a new excitement they climbed the stone steps and started exploring. "Do we know what we're looking for?" Jen asked.

"I'm thinking some kind of altar, showplace, something. I don't expect it to stand out," Max replied.

* * *

Six hours later they regrouped on the steps near the top.

"I expected it to be more, I don't know, touristy," Jen started. "I knew it was raw, but I still expected some roped off sections, maybe a gift shop at the entrance. I'm already worn out and we've only walked one pyramid. I didn't find anything."

Max and Lizard hadn't found anything either, but Max wasn't quite done with Structure Two. "I say we just walk around and put the codex down on any flat surface we can find." He was half joking. "The white pyramid just feels right. If I was a tourist I would start here."

"Maybe they started here, but found the codex somewhere else," Jen suggested. "The guide said they hiked all over for a couple of days."

"Uh guys, look out there." Lizard was insistent. She was pointing back at the dirt parking lot.

"Oh shit," Jen and Max said in unison. The Fist of Allah was piling out of a battered Chevy, carrying AK-47's. One of them pointed at the white pyramid. The others raised their AK's and started firing. Bullets pinged off of the pyramid as Jen, Lizard and Max ran back inside.

After the first turn, Lizard stopped them. "We'll never get out of here before those guys arrive. An AK-47 isn't accurate at this distance, but one guy can still cover most of the valley. You need to find a place to hide. I'll slip out and try to get around them."

"Don't you have a gun?" Jen asked.

"Yes, but I don't have an assault rifle. I'll have a better chance in close quarters. For now you need to hide so we can surprise them."

# 18.

HE HAD THEM IN HIS SIGHTS. THIS WAS the end. Omar could feel it. Allah would give them the codex and the means to shutdown air travel. They could isolate America while Islam marched on the rest of the world.

Beyond the pyramid, the sky was gray with ash. Omar could see the orange glow of the newly active volcano on the horizon. They would have to hurry. He left Kaseem to provide cover fire from the parking lot and headed down with Mohammed in tow.

Omar turned to Mohammed. "Don't kill all of them. We need at least one of them to tell us how to use the codex."

The place was deserted except for a park ranger who came running up, waiving at Omar and yelling at him in Spanish. Omar shot him at point blank range and took the man's flashlight from his belt.

They tried to move quickly, but the increasing level of ash in the air was making it hard to see and difficult to breathe.

The pyramid was a nightmare for the Fist of Allah. It was darker inside than Omar expected. Wasn't this some kind of tourist attraction? The structure was full of dark corners and places to hide. He'd left Mohammed outside in case his prey got past him, but now he had to search this whole place himself.

He tried a new tactic.

"Come out now and we won't hurt you. We just want the codex. If we have to hunt you down we will not be so merciful," he called. He didn't want to kill them...yet. He wanted the codex. He would prefer to have them alive, but he would have to figure out how to use the codex on his own if he had to. He worried that this was going to take all day.

Outside, the weather was getting worse. Mohammed could barely see. The volcano was spewing more ash into the sky. He heard something in the air, but he couldn't place it. His first thought was a helicopter, but no one could fly through this soup. Then he heard the gunshot, way out by the parking lot where Kaseem was. He wondered what Kaseem was shooting at.

Mohammed hoped that Omar would finish soon. He could hear noise from the volcano now. The eruptions were getting worse, and he was getting nervous. Through the gloom, a shape appeared. He wondered if it was a Jinn, roughly the Muslim equivalent of a ghost. Mohammed was an engineer, but the lack of sleep over the last few days had taken their toll and he fell back on the ancient superstitions his grandmother had taught him.

"Who is there?" he cried out.

"Put down your weapon," was the reply.

Mohammed fired blindly into the darkness. A boom that sounded like a cannon was the reply, and Mohammed's chest bloomed crimson.

Can you go to paradise if you are killed by a Jinn? He wondered idly as he slipped into death. He was about to find out.

It wasn't a Jinn that killed Mohammed. It was a Lizard, a Lizard with a Glock.

Lizard started to climb the steps of the white pyramid.

* * *

Inside the pyramid, Omar wasn't having any luck. He stopped in disgust. As the flashlight pointed down he saw fresh footprints and scuff marks in the layer of dirt covering the floor. Interesting, thought Omar. He followed the marks where they ended in a rock wall. It looked like part of the pyramid wall had caved in, but there were fresh markings at the base and a few loose rock lying around.

Omar cautiously moved a few stones. The wall wasn't solid. He had found their hiding place. Omar enlarged the opening and fired a three round burst into the hole. "Come out now and bring the codex," he bellowed.

Max and Jen crawled out of the hole and raised their hands. Max held the codex in one hand. Omar took it from him. He used the muzzle of the AK-47 to nudge them down the tunnel toward the opening at the top of the pyramid. He wanted more light to see the codex and then he would force them to tell him how to use it.

Jen looked at Max. His face was grim. She couldn't believe that they had come all this way to fail. Still, they were in a dark pyramid with a lot of steps down. Anything could happen.

The stepped out onto the platform at the top of the pyramid. The terrorist stopped them and turned them around. With their back to the pyramid steps and a gun pointed at them from the front they were running out of options. Behind them, it was a long way down.

The AK-47 shifted to point at Jen. The terrorist's stare didn't waver as he said to Max, "You will tell me how to use the codex or I will shoot the girl."

"Don't tell him Max." Jen's voice had an edge.

From down the pyramid steps she heard, "It's over asshole. You've lost. Put down the weapon and let them go."

Jen's hope returned. She risked a look back. It was Lizard pointing a handgun at them. She was about a third of the way down the steps on a wide platform that served to break up the pyramid's outline.

"Don't come any closer or I will shoot them, starting with the girl." Omar kept the gun on Jen, but turned his head toward Max. "Tell me how to use the codex," he insisted.

Max thought hard about all he knew about the Maya and all he had learned about Q'uq'umatz over the last several weeks.

"Don't tell him Max. He has no reason to keep you alive if he knows how to use it," Lizard yelled.

Max looked back at Lizard. Even at this distance, her handgun looked huge, but it was a long, uphill shot with a handgun. Plus he and Jen were between the terrorist and Lizard's Glock. He didn't have much choice.

Just then Jennifer spoke up. "Step out into the light and I'll show you how to use it." Jennifer had been thinking hard about the Maya too. She'd also been thinking about Max's earlier comment that they would have to trust Q'uq'umatz.

"No tricks." Omar's voice was firm.

"No tricks," Jen confirmed. "Trust me Max." She shot Max a look that she hoped he would understand, but she couldn't be sure that he got the message.

"Open the codex to the middle. Don't worry, you'll be able to understand it. We don't know why, but you can read it."

Omar awkwardly balanced the codex across the arm that was holding the AK-47. The volcano behind them rumbled again. Jen hoped that this would work.

"In the center, there is a curse. The sky god Q'uq'umatz declares death from above to anyone who disturbs his holy book. You have to read that section to activate the codex."

Omar eyed her suspiciously. He found the section and started to read. His voice rose in volume as he pronounced the curse with a shout. "Death from above to anyone who disturbs the book of Q'uq'u-matz."

Behind him, at the edge of the horizon, the volcano was belching fire now. Jen thought he looked like the devil with hell rising up behind. For a moment nothing happened. Max watched the horizon through the haze. Suddenly he understood what Jennifer was doing. He dove for her and they both started rolling down the steps. Only Lizard witnessed the flaming rock belched from the heart of the volcano that fell through the sky and obliterated Omar.

Max and Jen rolled to a stop on the platform with Lizard as she ducked down to avoid flaming debris.

Both Max and Jen groaned as they untangled themselves.

Jen sat up and looked at Max disgusted. "Next time warn me before you tackle me. What just happened?"

"You just harnessed the power of the sky god to kill a terrorist. I'm starting to wonder who the Mayan expert really is," Lizard replied, grinning.

Jen looked up and saw a flaming smudge where they had just been standing. "The codex!"

"Let's go and find it," Lizard said. "If it survived an airplane crash, it will survive a lava hit. I think Max may still have to figure out how to return it."

Max blinked. "Oh shit. You're right." He scrambled up the steps. Jen and Lizard followed at a slower pace. The codex was sitting on the platform where Omar had been standing. It looked as pristine as the day Jen had found it in the Fiesta Air crash.

Max picked up the codex and led them back inside. "I have an idea."

He took them to the chamber that they had hidden in. Max had seen something before they turned off the flashlight to hide.

This time, they made a huge hole. Everyone was too tired to crawl through a smaller one. They walked in and played their flashlights around the room. In the center of the room was a stone altar. The walls were decorated with pictographs of the city, Q'uq'umatz, and ritual sacrifices. A skeleton lay against the wall with a stone knife protruding from its breast.

"I caught a glimpse of the walls as we crawled in here," Max started. "I believe that this is the sacred chamber of the Mayan sky god Q'uq'umatz."

"How did the Raintrees get in here?" Jen asked.

"It had to be one or both of the kids," Max answered. "What we know about the parents would suggest that they wouldn't take an artifact like a book. I think the kids found the chamber and stole the codex."

Lizard turned from examining a pictograph on the wall. "What do we do now? How do we return the book?"

"More importantly, how do we keep other people from finding it?" asked Jen.

"I think we need to put the book back on the altar and, if I'm right, Q'uq'umatz will figure out how to protect the book."

"You're the Mayan expert. Do we need to say something too?" Jen asked.

Max stepped forward and formally addressed the altar. "Oh great Q'uq'umatz. Please accept this return of your sacred text."

Jen giggled at his awkward speech as Max laid the codex on the center of the altar. Through the pyramid walls they heard the boom of the volcano erupting. The ground beneath the pyramid shook.

The trio looked at each other. With a flat tone and no emotion in her voice, Lizard said, "run."

They ran. The little group sprinted out of the chamber, up through the platform entrance and down what seemed like a million steps. The sky rained ash and bits of sulfur. A wicked wind whipped the ash into little gritty missiles. All the while, the earth continued to shake.

"Run for the parking lot," Lizard yelled.

Jen ran remembering all of those jogs through Atlanta and cursing all of the times she had skipped them lately. Max wasn't in nearly as good shape and he lagged behind, breathing heavily.

Just past the car park, on a flat piece of ground, sat a dark Blackhawk helicopter. It had been a gift to the Mexican Army from the U.S. in their war against the drug cartels. The Blackhawk's rotors were spinning and it was starting to take off. Lizard pointed her Glock at the pilot and yelled "Halto." She didn't know if the pilot heard her, but the chopper settled back down to the ground. Jen couldn't figure out how the special agent could run fast enough to beat her there, but right now, she didn't care.

Max finally ran up, red faced and looking like he was going to have a heart attack. Lizard dragged him into the chopper and screamed "Go, go, go, rapido!"

The chopper controls were mushy in the ash-laden air, but they got off and flew straight east running from the volcano. Eventually they turned north to head back to Mexico proper. Out the open door the trio watched as the white pyramid of Calakmul was buried in a shower of flaming rock tossed by the volcano.

# Epilogue

I T TOOK SEVERAL DAYS OF DIPLOMATIC untangling to get them out of Mexico. Max and Jen had entered the country illegally, a Mexican Navy boat had been sunk, and a national treasure was buried in lava and ash. The Mexican Federales evacuated the tourists from Cancun not long after the Fist of Allah left for Calakmul. Captain Jack had gone with them and was now resting comfortably at home in New Orleans.

Once back in the U.S., Jen and Max had been ordered not to leave Atlanta. They were still facing charges of interfering with a federal investigation and evidence tampering.

Lizard met with the President and his national security advisor in the Oval Office. After she finished her briefing, the President asked, "so are you sure that this over?"

"Yes sir. The original codex was returned and is now buried under hardening lava. All of the copies have mysteriously disappeared, including the ones in evidence. The would-be terrorists are dead except for the one you have in custody. All that's left is for you to drop the charges against Max and Jen. It's the right thing to do and you know it."

The national security advisor piped up. "So we just let this whole thing go down as terrorism? Calling this a terrorist incident could hurt the President's reelection chances."

"Well we can't very well tell the country that a sacred Mayan codex was behind the crashes. That would end the President's chances at re-election." Lizard sat back with her arms crossed and a defiant look on her face.

The President turned to his national security advisor. "No, she's right. I'll ask the attorney general to drop the charges. The FBI isn't going to let this go without my intervention. They are dying to arrest somebody, but I'll make them see the light. As for the election, we'll manage our way through that."

\* \* \*

In Jen's apartment, Max and Jen laid in a tangle on the couch watching the news.

"In a dramatic turn of events, the historic Mayan site of Calakmul was covered by an unusual lava flow from a recently active Mexican volcano." The reporter tried to look dismayed. "You'll remember that this is the site where authorities claim that the terrorists responsible for the recent airliner attacks were killed. Archeologists are already promising to excavate the site once the lava cools."

Max looked at Jen. "I guess old Q'uq'umatz found a way to hide his codex after all."

"Yeah, let hopes he hides it for a long, long time."

# ABOUT THE AUTHOR

Mark Polino is a CPA and accounting software consultant. After spending way too much time on airplanes he felt the need to crash a few, on paper of course.

Mark lives in Florida with his family and an undisclosed number of dogs.

www.mpolino.com

bit.ly/mpolinoauthor